These Paper Walls
Book 4 in the My Paper Heart Saga
Magan Vernon

For information visit www.maganvernon.com

Summary: Starting a life and family? Check

Getting Offers for higher paying jobs? Check

Turning down a hottie from the past...Um...not so much.

Blaine Crabtree never considered himself a lucky man until Libby Gentry came into his life.

Now, he isn't sure if he is lucky or just the biggest sap in the parish.

To be fair, he is a married man now with a baby on the way, but that doesn't stop old habits from dying hard.

With his friends calling for him to go out and a job relocation out of town, he isn't getting to see much of Libby, but a certain ex keeps finding her way back to him.

When Blaine feels like the walls are closing in around him, will he break out and go on his own path or are he and Libby meant to be?

First Edition, October 2015

Cover Design by Sharp Cover Designs

http://www.sharpcoverdesign.com/

Cover photography by Michael Meadows Studios

http://www.michaelmeadowsstudios.com/

Cover model: Brandon Lane

https://www.facebook.com/Brandonromance2846

Edited by Kellie Montgomery at Eye Candy Bookstore

http://www.eyecandybookstore.com/

To Alissa
Without you, I wouldn't be able to write these stories. To do all that I do. You're my right hand and the ying to my yang. Best assistant and author duo ever!

Praise for The My Paper Heart Saga

[Vernon] is an eloquent writer and knows how to really develop her characters! I look forward to more of her work! - Heather at Nightly Reading Reviews

Her sassy female lead, Libby, puts the 'fun' in funny and makes *My Paper Heart* an extremely entertaining read!- *Candace at Lovey Dovey Books*

I really enjoyed this story of finding love and discovering who you truly are. - *Laura at Bookish Treasers on My Paper Heart*

I love Magan's honest style of writing. Her characters have flaws and make mistakes. And her love scenes are a mix of sexy and sometimes hilariously awkward!

- Amy at The Reading Realm on On Paper Wings

I love a book that stays with you even when it's over. Blaine and Libby's unconditional love left an unforgettable trail on my heart! A must read!

- Heather at Books, Chocolate, and Lipgloss on A Paper Trail

Prologue

One Year Ago

"Come on Crabtree, you can't tell me you still think LSU is going to pull through this season." Butch Sinclair chugged the last of his beer and then threw it on the floor.

It felt like we did the same thing every single night: went to Jackson's parents' place, drank, and then Butch and Jackson argued with me about LSU. Not like there was much else to do in Small town, USA. We either hung out at the trailer and some random girl took me into her backseat, or I stayed home and waited for another girl to call. My life was what some guys dreamed about, but honestly, it was getting real old, real fast.

I laughed. "And you really think Ole Miss can do shit? You're crazy."

"Crazy as that night you did Layla Duggar in the church parking lot?" Jackson elbowed me in the side then him and Butch cackled like two hyenas in heat.

Once they were done with their laughing fit, Butch looked up and his eyes practically bugged out of his head like a cartoon character. "I see something I'd like to bang in any parking lot."

My eyes trailed up, way up a pair of long, tanned legs to what Butch was staring at. Or should I say who. I'd never seen the girl before and I would have know; not only is Elsbury tiny, but she was the most beautiful girl I'd ever seen. I couldn't have missed her. Ever. She was wearing nothing but a short skirt and a tiny white tank top that hugged every inch of her curves. Long, blonde curls traveled down her back and all I could think about was running my fingers through her hair while she wrapped those legs around me.

Then it was as if time stopped. Her chocolate brown eyes locked on mine and everyone else in the room disappeared. It was just me and those eyes. It sounds cheesy as hell, but right there, I saw my future with her. She wasn't just another girl that I wanted to bang, but I wanted to talk to her. Buy her flowers. Take her to meet my mom. Have her be the one walking down the aisle toward me. People tell me love at first sight is just a crock of shit, but when I saw those eyes, I knew they were wrong.

She broke our stare down, biting her bottom lip and looking at the floor before Jackson's sister and Dee Badeaux's granddaughter, Brittany, started talking to her again. They were like two hens in a hen house flapping around her.

"Who is that?" I glanced at Butch, who was licking his lips and straightening out his trucker cap.

It was Jackson who answered. "That's Dee Badeaux's niece, Libby Gentry. She failed out of college so her parents sent her down here to get some Southern learning and straighten her out."

"I'd like to straighten her out with my dick." Butch clicked his teeth, staring at her like she was a piece of meat.

I opened my mouth to say something, but then the beginning of "Pour some sugar on me" blared through the speakers. Butch's jaw practically dropped to the floor and I followed his gaze. There was Libby, swaying her body to the beat of the music and trying to pull Brittany along with her. She moved her long legs to the floor and back up again, her ass practically staring me in the face. I felt my jeans tighten. The girl could definitely move.

"Well, it looks like it shouldn't be too hard to do that. Looks like I'm getting lucky tonight." Butch wiped his mouth.

I couldn't let him try. I couldn't let him spoil the one ray of sunshine I thought could possibly poke into my life. I had to get to her first, and not let her end up being some conquest of any other guy. I knew at that moment that I wanted Libby Gentry to be mine.

"The hell you are." I shot up from the couch and ran over to the blonde goddess. Her back was to me, but I could already smell her shampoo or perfume. Whatever it was, it smelled like summertime: sunshine and strawberries, and I had to adjust myself again before I grabbed onto her arm and stopped her dancing. If I didn't end up with her that night, I didn't want anyone else to. The moment I met her, I fell in love with her and if I had to make her hate me first, then so be it.

"What the hell do you think you're doing?"

Chapter One

Present Day

I couldn't sleep.

Don't get me wrong, I was tired as hell from working my ass off all day on the road crew, but the further Libby got into her pregnancy, the more uncomfortable she got in bed.

I'd dreamt of sharing a bed with her. I had all these fantasies that didn't involve a giant pregnancy pillow in my face or all of the covers on the floor.

Since sleeping wasn't an option, I got up early and started working in the kitchen.

I'd always been set to inherit my meemaw's house, I just didn't think it would be so soon, or that it would need a shit ton of work, especially when my new wife wanted a lot of upgrades.

I'm not saying Libby was spoiled, but the girl had a champagne wish list and we were working on a cheap beer budget.

At least knocking down some cabinets early in the morning was a way to work off some steam.

I'd just gotten the last of the upper cabinets down when I turned around to see Libby standing in the middle of the hardwood floor, wiping her eyes. I'd have to say, even at seven months pregnant, the girl was still gorgeous. Instead of looking heavy, she had curves that filled out every inch of her little nightgown. But with the scowl on her face, I had a feeling that she wasn't standing in the kitchen, hoping to fulfill some counter sex fantasy.

"What are you doing? Do you know what time it is?" she asked.

"I'm just knocking down these cabinets so Dad and I can get working on the new floating shelves to replace them. I think it'll look real nice once we get it painted and the tile backsplash up." I rubbed the now bare wall.

"And you think it's a good idea to do that at five in the morning? Lucky we don't have neighbors or I'm sure they'd go all Disturbia on us and think we'd murdered someone."

I shook my head. "I think you're using the wrong reference, but I get what you mean. I'll stop. I should get ready for work anyway."

"Yeah, I have classes today. Did you call the internet guy again to see if he can come out here? I really hate having to go to Aunt Dee's to work on school stuff."

I winced. No, I didn't call him, I was busy working my ass of everyday in the blistering Louisiana sun while she sat with her feet up. Okay, so it was dickish of me to complain. She was pregnant, like really pregnant. I couldn't imagine what that was like. "No, I haven't. Do you want to try calling them today?"

She blinked then nodded. "Okay. Yeah. I guess I can do that."

I wiped my face with a towel; I was already dripping in sweat, but hardly noticed it. It was a hazard of always working outside in the bayou heat. "I guess I'll go shower now that you're up. Want to make me breakfast?"

She smiled, raising an eyebrow. "You mean pour your cereal and milk in a bowl since we still don't have a working stove?"

"Hey, Meemaw never complained about using the toaster oven."

Libby shook her head. "I don't know if your Meemaw used the stovetop for anything other than lighting her cigarettes, which was probably really scary when you think about it. You know, since she was always attached to that oxygen tank."

I shrugged. "Meemaw was Meemaw."

"So...does this mean we can go appliance shopping soon?" She chewed on her bottom lip, which always got me going. There was something about the little nip at that plump pink skin that made me have to adjust myself.

I put my arms around her and pulled her close. "Soon, baby. I promise. We've got other things we need to take care of first."

She traced the lines of my bicep. "You know...if we did need the extra money..."

I stepped back, shaking my head. "I thought we agreed on this? We don't need to be asking your parents for money. I get paid next week and you should start getting paid from Dee soon. We can maybe talk about using some of that for a new stove."

She sighed. We'd had the same argument hundreds of times. I expected her to put up more of a fight but instead she just yawned. "Okay. We'll talk later then."

THE PARISH WAS WIDENING one of the many two lane roads that headed out of Elsbury and into New Orleans. We'd been working on it for a few weeks and it looked like it was going to get done, which meant finally getting paid.

Then I wouldn't have to ask Libby's dad for money.

Not that I'd thought about it.

Okay, I'd thought about it occasionally, but the guy thought I was the biggest piece of shit on the planet. I could still remember the moment I called him to ask for Libby's hand.

"Dr. Gentry." His voice was arrogant. Snooty. It was the kind of voice that CEOs always had in bad movies.

I swallowed hard. "Hi, Mr. Gentry, sir, it's Blaine Crabtree, Libby's boyfriend."

I somehow just knew he had that cocky smirk on his face. Maybe it was because he did that like 'hmph' thing that guys like him tended to do.

"Well, I can't say I was expecting your call. I thought you might have run over state lines by now."

So I guess Libby told him...

"No, sir, I wouldn't do that."

"Really? Because last time I had an upset phone call from my daughter it was because you broke her heart. Now I find out that after sending her down to live with her aunt to grow up and continue her education, she's pregnant. Pregnant with your child I assume. What are you going to do about that?"

I scratched the back of my neck, my hand trembling. I never backed down from a challenge, but there was something about the guy that intimidated the hell out of me, especially when I was about to ask him something really important. "Well, sir, I was hoping I could get your blessing to ask Libby to marry me."

He laughed but there was no humor in it. "You think that's what my daughter needs? Do you really think you can provide for her? A guy that still lives with his parents and works on some road crew in a Podunk Louisiana town?"

I clenched my fists, counting backwards from ten. This was the same thought that had been plaguing me since the moment I met Libby. I never thought I was good enough for her and now I had confirmation that her dad knew it.

"Well sir, I can sure as hell try."

When I pulled up to the site, my buddy Jackson was already there, so I parked next to him.

"Hey man," I said as I got out of my SUV. I missed my truck. I missed it a lot. It was the first thing I ever bought myself that was a big ticket item, but I needed something that could fit a family in.

"Hey, Crabtree, you talk to the foreman yet?" Jackson had a full red beard and bright red hair. When he wore the yellow work vest he looked like some kind of cartoon character.

"No, not yet."

Jackson nodded. "He's already given me my new assignment. Potholes off Main. Shitty little few week job, but it could be worse."

"Yeah, at least you'll be close to home and near Dina's work. You could probably stop in for a quickie every day."

He laughed and smacked my back. "Yeah, maybe you'll get the same thing. How is pregnant sex anyway? Feel different down there?"

"Why the hell do you want to hear about my wife's parts, man?"

He shrugged. "Hey, a guy's gotta ask."

I shook my head. "She's fine. We're fine."

Jackson cocked an eyebrow. "You don't sound fine, man. Everything okay?"

"Yeah. I'm good."

"So, she's going to let you off the leash and you can meet some of us for drinks after work?"

I licked my lips and smirked. "Naw, man. I gotta head home."

He laughed, smacking his knee. "I knew you were whipped. What's Libby want you to do now? Go shopping for more baby stuff? Maybe install some fancy new granite in your Meemaw's bathroom?"

He was half right. We were going to go look at new countertops to install with my dad, but I wasn't about to tell him that, so I just patted him on the back. "I'm going to go see the foreman."

Daniel Vance was the kind of no-shit-taking man that just looking at him, you knew he did some time. He was talking to one of the other guys, looking through some papers attached to a clipboard.

He gave me a nod then patted the guy on the back before he took off. "Blaine, Jackson tell ya I was looking for you?"

I nodded and stepped closer. "Yes, sir."

He smiled. The guy looked like an older, tattooed version of Santa. I had a feeling that beneath the crude tattoos and hard exterior, he may be a teddy bear. "This project is set to end Friday. You ready for the next one?"

"Yes, sir."

"Good. You know you've always been one of my best workers. You're young, take initiative, and I'm expecting that in a few years when your back's about to give out, you'll be in for my job."

"Wow, thank you, sir. That's an honor."

He flipped through his papers. "And it's because of your hard work and dedication that I put you in for the Crescent City Connection job."

I widened my eyes. "The one in New Orleans?"

He smiled. "The very one. It's a big opportunity. Any of these guys would kill to get their hands on that project."

Yeah and I normally would have too, but that was almost an hour away, on a good day. With traffic, it could be an hour and a half.

I rubbed the back of my neck. "That seems like a great opportunity sir, but it is kind of far out from Elsbury."

Daniel put his big bear paw on my shoulder. "Son, I know you have the new wife and baby on the way. Don't you want to do something that's going to provide for their future?"

I swallowed hard. There was no way in hell I could say no to this, even if I was afraid of what Libby was going to say about it.

Chapter 2

By the time I got off work for the day I was dead tired. I thought maybe I'd get to see Libby before she went off to her summer night class, but when I pulled up to the house, it was dark.

She only had another week of this class then she would be done, but, of course, she signed up for another set of classes in August. I felt like the only time I ever saw her was when we crashed into bed at night.

I guess it wasn't all bad. She'd be done by the end of August and then be home for a semester with the baby. And, by her not being home at that moment, I had more time to think about how the hell I was going to tell her that I was going to be away from home even more.

I walked inside the house and as the cold air hit my face, my eyes immediately started to drift. I never went inside while I was working because I knew how the cold air had that effect on me.

I set my keys down on the table and walked into the living room. We still didn't have much for furniture, since we decided to donate my Meemaw's. I would have kept it, but Libby complained that the floral print was outdated. That, and Meemaw died on her old chair. I guess it was better to get rid of it than to have bad Gris Gris.

The only thing we had in the living room was a set of outdoor folding chairs that I used for tailgating. I kept telling myself that we'd get new furniture after I refinished the wood floor and painted, but now I was wondering if I'd ever finish the floor or paint...or have the money to buy furniture.

I sighed and slumped down on one of the chairs, facing the old brick fireplace. *That needed to be fixed as well.* I ran my hands over my face and shook my head. "When the hell am I going to get this all done and have the money to do it?"

I could keep staying up every night and work on it, but if my drooping eyelids were any indication, that wasn't going to work.

Maybe this new job would bring in some money. Maybe this week I'd get paid more than I thought and I could surprise Libby with a trip to Elsbury Furniture and let her pick out a sofa set.

Or maybe I would just sleep...

"BLAINE? BLAINE?"

The bright light hit my eyes and I squinted, opening them slowly to see Libby leaning over me and examining me as if I were some sort of science experiment. "Were you seriously passed out?"

I shook my head, rubbing my eyes. "No. I mean. Yes. I mean. What the hell time is it anyway?"

She raised an eyebrow. "It's eleven. I thought I'd find you in bed by now. Are you okay?"

Shit. Did I really sleep for that long?

"Yeah, I'm fine. Just tired I guess."

She folded her arms across her chest, frowning. "Well, at least you're almost done with this job. Dina said that Jackson got some breezy job filling potholes on Main. Did you get your new assignment, too?"

I tried not to wince. I didn't want to have this conversation. Not when I was half asleep and really not ever. "No, not yet. Hopefully tomorrow."

She dropped her hands and nodded. "Good. Hopefully it's a good one."

I stood up. "Yeah, I guess we could use a break."

"Are you going to come to come to bed with me?" she asked, twirling a strand of her blonde hair around her finger.

I smiled. "Well, I guess being with you in bed is better than this chair."

She put her hand out and I took it, getting out of the chair and following her to the bedroom. It was the only room of the house we really did any updating to and that wasn't by choice. Instead of using our wedding money for a honeymoon or anything else spectacular, we found out that we had major plumbing issues in the master bathroom. We only found that out because we tried taking a shower after the wedding and have a little romance, but only ended up with a fallen shower head and water dripping from the ceiling in the bedroom.

But at least now it was sort of an oasis, when everything else was crumbling in the house. We painted the walls a light gray that complimented the old white wainscoting and wooden beams on the ceiling. I even had to admit that the yellow bedding set that Libby made us register for made my old bed look a little more adult.

"Do you want to take a shower with me?" Libby asked, raising an eyebrow.

"Are you saying I smell?"

She pulled me closer, biting down on her bottom lip. "You smell fine, but I smell like a pregnant woman that has been sweating in the late June heat and need one, so you can join me or not."

I looped my arms around her waist and splayed my hands across her lower back, ever slowly guiding my fingers up, relishing in the feel of her warm skin under her shirt. "I'd love nothing more than to see you wet."

She giggled, biting down on that lip even harder. I responded by kissing her fiercely. She could turn me on with just one look and it had been a while since we'd been anything close to intimate.

I broke the kiss slightly, only to pull her shirt over her head and then toss mine aside as well. She pulled me back to her, capturing my bottom lip in her teeth, which caused me to moan before licking her lips and kissing her again. She pressed her body to mine; even pregnant, her skin felt amazing against me. Every little move of her hands set my body on fire and I wanted her naked as soon as possible.

Libby must have been thinking the same thing because she broke the kiss only to loop her fingers through my belt loops and walk backwards, pulling me into the bathroom until she stopped at the shower. We'd gotten rid of Meemaw's old tub when the bathroom flooded, so now we had a larger walk in shower with a seat. Libby said it would be great for baby bathing, but I just thought about shower sex.

She let go of my belt loops and slowly peeled off her shorts and underwear. No matter how many times I'd seen her naked, and even with her growing belly, she still turned me on with all of her tanned skin and the new curves of her hips and chest. Maybe she'd let me finally grab the new boobs if I got her in the shower.

She turned away from me and turned on the water, so I shucked off my pants and underwear as quickly as I could before pressing into her back and looping my arms around her waist. I kissed a line from her neck down her shoulders. She tilted her head back and put her hand to my face, grinding her butt into my groin as she moaned.

If I wasn't already hard, I was more than ready, feeling all of her against me.

Just when I thought she might turn around to get closer, she stepped forward and into the shower.

"Awww, come on, baby!" I groaned.

She smiled and tugged my arm until I fell forward, catching myself on the glass wall before closing the door behind us. The waterfall showerhead fell over us, heating up my sore muscles that I didn't even know were sore until I started moving. But it was hard to concentrate on anything else when Libby moved her wet hair from her face as droplets fell down her lips and to the curve of her breast.

I couldn't help myself as I leaned forward and licked each falling drop from her breast and swirled my tongue around her nipple. Libby moaned in response, arching her back and digging her core into me. I glanced up to see her eyes closed and damn if she wasn't biting on that bottom lip again.

This was the most she'd let me touch her since our wedding and damn if I wasn't going to take advantage of every part of it. With a tentative hand, I trailed my fingers down the curve of her hip and then tip-toed to her center, running my thumb down her sensitive flesh before curving a finger inside of her.

She cried out, bucking her hips forward over and over again until she was coming hard on my finger.

I smiled, licking my way up her breast to her collarbone and neck until my lips were at her ear. "I need to be inside of you, now," I growled.

She responded by pushing my fingers deeper into her and crying out again.

Slowly, I moved my hand and she whimpered softly, as if she was already missing the loss of having me inside her. But that wasn't going to last long. I grabbed her thigh and moved her leg to the shower bench. I kept my other hand firmly on her other leg, before slowly pushing my way inside of her.

Before she got pregnant, well except for the time we didn't, we'd always been careful. Always used protection. Now there was no need for it and damn, feeling every part of her on me made it hard to last, especially when she was so wet, so ready.

I held onto her thigh with one hand and splayed my other one on the shower wall beside her head, moving my lips to hers and kissing her deeply. She moaned into my mouth as I slowly thrusted inside of her while her hands gripped firmly onto my ass.

She felt amazing. With the water dripping over us she was glistening and the little sounds that escaped her mouth into mine made my whole body ripple with pleasure. She clenched around me as I felt her body shake again and she tilted her head back as she came hard around me and I followed soon after.

We stood there for a minute, just holding each other as the water fell over us. I didn't want to move. I just wanted to stay in that moment forever.

But just like our future, things were going to change and I couldn't hold onto things.

"Need me to help you get washed up?" she asked, staring at me with a large grin on her face.

I laughed. "Always."

Chapter 3

I should have probably told Libby about the new job, but after she scrubbed me down in the shower and I returned the favor, it was past midnight and I passed the hell out, only to get up again in a few hours to get ready for work.

At least I only had a few days left before the Fourth of July holiday.

A year ago, Libby and I had gotten into one of the biggest fights of our relationship on the Fourth. One that was half my fault, okay, mostly my fault. I hoped that wasn't what she always thought about on the Fourth. Or my even bigger fuck up in our relationship.

"She loves you, you fucking idiot. She told you that she loved you and you fought with her and came running here instead of saying it back?"

"I know. I know. I'm a dumbass." I ran my hand over my face.

Jackson and I stood in his kitchen. He was in the middle of cooking dinner, but turned off the burner and handed me a beer as soon as I walked in.

I should have just turned back around and gone to Libby's or done something, but instead I found myself driving down the gravel path to Jackson's place.

"Well, what the hell are you going to do about it? Ain't you supposed to fly to Chicago with her tomorrow?"

I took a long pull of my beer. "Yeah. That's probably not going to happen."

Jackson raised his eyebrows. "So you're going to break the girl's heart again? That sounds like a major dick move, even for you."

I shook my head. "You know I ain't never going to be good enough for her. She can't fall in love with me, you know as well as I do that nothing good is going to come of her staying with me."

"Then why do you stay with her? Why, if you seem to think that this is a bad idea, do you stay with her?"

I raked my fingers through my hair. "I don't know! Maybe I'm stupid? A glutton for punishment."

Jackson pointed his beer at me. "Or maybe you love her too and that scares the shit out of you."

I blew out a deep breath. "I don't even know what the hell love is."

He shook his head. "I think love is different for each person, but I think the one thing it has in common is putting the other person's feelings before yours. If you're so worried about Libby loving you, isn't that the same thing?"

I shook my head. "Don't get all philosophical on me right now, Jacks."

He put his hands up. "I'm just saying. I've seen the way you are with her. You know you love her, I just wish you weren't so stupid and you'd put down your beer and drive back over there to apologize."

"We both know I'm not going to do that."

He set his beer down on the counter and crossed his arms over his chest. "Then what are you going to do? Are you going to completely break this girl's heart? Go home and maybe call up one of your past hussies to see if they'll help you get over her, but you know they won't? Why don't you just man up, buddy, for once in your life."

"Fuck you, Jackson," I spat.

"No need to resort to language. I'm just telling you the truth."

"Thanks for the beer," I muttered, setting the half-empty bottle down on the counter before turning and walking out of his house.

He didn't follow. He didn't say anything else. He just let me think on his words.

I lay in bed, unable to sleep, just staring at the ceiling. The same ceiling that not long ago I'm sure Libby had been staring at when I was inside of her.

Now I was alone. Really alone.

And I missed her. I fucking missed her. I missed the way her hair fell over face. The way she bit her lip when she was nervous. Everything.

I shut my eyes, trying to block out her smile, but I couldn't. There was no way to block her out.

I was fucking in love with Libby Gentry, which was dangerous.

I'd seen the hotel her friend was getting married at. I looked up the suburb her parents lived in. They were millionaires and I was just a redneck from southern Louisiana. I'd never be enough.

I shook my head. The best thing was just to end this now before either of us got hurt anymore than we already were.

I somehow managed to pass out and not wake up until my alarm went off. Maybe it was because Libby gave me a workout in the shower, or maybe it was because I tried to completely shut off my brain.

Granted, I should have told Libby about the new job, but with her lying on my chest, her blonde hair splayed on the pillow next to me, I didn't want to do anything to disturb her.

I took another shower, got dressed, and made some coffee all without Libby ever waking up. We had a set of French doors that led out back where the wrap-around porch met our backyard. I opened the door and stepped outside. I had mowed Meemaw's lawn for as long as I could remember. It wasn't a huge yard, but it was surrounded by weeping willows that always provided enough shade so I wasn't dying in the summer heat.

The sun hadn't risen yet, so the yard was still dark. It was calm. Almost peaceful.

I had a few minutes before I had to leave for work. I could have started working on something in the living room, but instead I took a seat on the back porch steps and sipped my coffee.

My eyes trailed to the trees at the end of the yard where the branches slowly swayed. A buck appeared. One of the biggest I'd ever seen.

It wasn't deer hunting season, but like hell I was going to let something like that go to waste.

Slowly, I set my coffee cup down and stood up, keeping my eyes on the deer. He barely moved, just bent his head down ever so slightly, then looked each way.

I kept my eyes on him, creeping into the house, then going in a full sprint to the hall closet where I grabbed my shotgun and a few shells. I ran back out to the back porch, half-expecting the deer to have fled, but he was still there. It was like he was waiting for me.

My adrenaline kicked in and my hands were shaking as I loaded the gun.

"Get your shit together, Crabtree. It hasn't been that long since you've shot anything."

But it had been. I didn't go hunting last fall and I knew I probably wouldn't be again for awhile. This might have been my only chance to get a deer.

I steadied my arm and aimed for the deer, squinting one eye, and zeroing in on him as I steadied my breath, resting my hand on the trigger.

One breath in and shoot on the way out.

In.

"What the hell do you think you're doing?"

I shot and missed completely, my breath catching in my throat before I turned around to see a wide-eyed Libby staring back at me.

I glanced back to see the deer running into the woods, then I looked back at Libby. "Dammit, you made me miss!"

"Are you trying to shoot a deer off our back porch? What the hell?"

I turned the safety on and set my gun down. "Yeah. That was at least a five pointer, maybe six. We could have gotten enough meat from him to last us months! We wouldn't have had to worry about food at all when the baby got here."

She frowned. "Because your first thought was the baby when you shot a giant gun off our back porch? What if it wasn't me behind you? What if our son crawled up your leg and you misfired and shot him?"

I shook my head and let out a deep breath out of my nose. "Baby, that wouldn't happen. I know what I'm doing."

She crossed her arms over her chest and kept the scowl on her face. "But you've never had a baby; you don't know what he could do. Hell, we haven't even picked a name for him yet and instead you're off trying to kill him a deer."

I arched an eyebrow. "What the hell does his name have to do with anything?"

She groaned and threw her arms up in the air. "Ugh! You don't get it at all! All you care about is what is in it for you when it comes to our family."

I growled. "What the hell are you talking about? I work my ass off five days a week in the sweltering heat to provide us a paycheck. Then, when I'm not working my regular job, I'm here, working on this house so it's in the best condition."

"Yeah, and you don't have to be working on the house. You know we could hire someone and have it done within a few weeks."

I groaned, feeling all the tension build up in my arms and my neck. "And who the hell is going to pay for us to get in some workers? You? Are you going to use some of your minimum wage paycheck from Dee's shop?"

She narrowed her eyes. "Maybe I will."

I laughed, even though it wasn't funny, but I couldn't stop. My chest tightened and I could barely breathe as I bent over.

"It's not funny! God, you're such an asshole!" she screeched before opening the door and slamming it behind her.

"Baby! Wait!" I opened the door and followed her, but was only greeted with our bedroom door shutting in my face.

"Libby...I'm sorry...come on, open up." I knocked, but she didn't answer, so I knocked again.

I glanced at the time on the big grandfather clock. I had to leave soon, but I didn't want to leave angry. "Come on, baby, at least come out and give me a goodbye kiss."

Still no answer.

I waited as long as I could. Even five minutes later than I would have normally left, but she didn't come out.

"Okay, baby, I'm leaving now. I'll be home around three, then we can talk."

I watched the door, walking backwards, even pausing when I was on the front porch. But the bedroom door didn't open and I left for work with a very angry wife.

Chapter 4

"**M**an, you look like shit," Jackson said as soon as I walked up to the site.

"Thanks, man, you don't look so great either," I grumbled.

He put his hands up. "Hey, just saying, maybe you should try to get some sleep in before the baby comes. Or if you ain't sleeping anyway, you could come out with me and some of the guys tomorrow night."

I raised an eyebrow. "How the hell is that going to help me?"

Jackson shrugged. "I don't know, but it couldn't hurt. Ever since you found out Libby was pregnant, you haven't hung out with us once. Hell, even before that you've been so puppy-dog whipped that we barely saw you."

I shoved his shoulder. "I'm not fucking whipped, man."

He put his arms up. "I'm just saying, it would be nice to see you once in a while."

I licked my lips. "Yeah. I'll think about it. Maybe a quick game of pool or something after work at Reesey's."

"That's my boy." Jackson slapped me on the back.

I couldn't remember the last time I'd been to Reesey's, or hung out with the boys, but I distinctly remembered the last time I was there with Libby and the guys.

"Another draft and a rum and Coke, Sadie." I leaned on the rickety bar, handing a twenty to the tattoo and hickey covered woman behind it. She was my oldest sister's age, but looked more like my meemaw.

Sadie nodded and pulled out two glasses. "That little city girl of yours can't handle the ghost?" she asked, filling up a glass with Ghost In The Machine, one of my favorite local IPAs.

I shook my head and smiled. "Naw, I think she may be hitting her limit. Maybe give her more Coke than rum."

Sadie filled up the glass and set it on the counter, looking over me. "Maybe she just needs some water, I think your girl may be about to get in a cat fight."

I turned toward where Sadie's eyes landed and saw Libby, swaying and leaning over a table. When I moved slightly to the left, my breath caught in my throat and it felt like all the air had been whooshed out of my lungs.

Julie.

My ex-girlfriend.

The one who ruined me.

I'd seen her earlier. The same girl who said she'd never set foot back in this Podunk town was now at my crew's hangout. Not only that, but she was talking to my girlfriend.

Before I could even approach them to see what the hell was going on, Libby turned around and staggered before her eyes fluttered and she hit the ground.

A crowd quickly gathered around her, but I pushed through them, kneeling down beside her. I thought she might have passed out, but she was still moaning and moving slightly. At least she was still conscious. I thought a sorority girl could probably drink me under the table, but I was wrong. Not everyone fit into their stereotypes, I guess, and that wasn't a bad thing. I didn't need a girl who was a drunk, but it would have been nice if she wasn't a rag doll.

"Someone needs to get this girl to a hospital," a random voice yelled.

"I'll take care of it," I grumbled, slowly helping her to a sitting position.

"Wow, Blaine, really moving up in the world."

I cringed, hearing Julie's voice. It used to be the voice that made my stomach do somersaults, now it just brought out a bunch of knots.

I put Libby's arm around my shoulder and slowly brought her to a standing position before turning to face Julie.

Julie was her usual prim and proper Southern belle self with her hair not a stitch out of place and the usual tease with her tanned cleavage on full display. But that wasn't what I was staring at. It was the scowl on her face. The one that was always there. The one that disapproved of everything I did, like I would never be good enough.

"Yeah, maybe she's had too much to drink. I'm going to take her home."

Julie nodded. "Yeah. That's probably a good idea."

I should have said something smart back. I should have asked why the hell she was even there, but instead I turned around and walked Libby out of the bar and into my truck.

I got Libby in with a little bit of effort and buckled her in as she leaned against the seat. She looked like she was sleeping peacefully with her head on the window instead of like she just passed the hell out.

I turned on my truck and headed toward town.

I should have taken her to the hospital or maybe called someone, but instead I found myself turning down a back road and pulling to the side of the road.

I hadn't smoked in forever. Libby didn't like it, but at that moment I needed something to calm my nerves. I cut the engine and rolled down the windows before pulling a pack of cloves out of my center console along with a lighter.

I sucked in the sweet taste of clove and nicotine and blew it out.

Fuck.

What the hell had I gotten myself into?

Once upon a time I thought Julie was my be all, end all.

We had grown up together. I'd watched her go from the gap-toothed girl on the monkey bars to the head cheerleader. She was my first everything. But she gave it up. As soon as she went away to college, she was done. It was like I was just another stepping stone on her life to being a future Stepford wife.

The night before she left for Ole Miss, I had a ring in my pocket. I didn't know if I wanted to get married then and I probably dodged one hell of a bullet by not pulling it out.

I just didn't want her to leave. All I'd known in life had been Elsbury, baseball, and Julie. Then she left. Guys usually didn't talk about things like heartbreak, but the girl fucked me up.

Libby stirred in the seat next to me and moaned softly. The moonlight shown in from the front windshield and bathed her in a soft glow. This beautiful girl was with me. This girl went and tried to stand up to the girl that fucked me over. Something I didn't even think was possible.

It may have been a dumbass move, but there was something I admired about it. She was willing to go the extra mile for me, something Julie would have never done.

Shit, I knew I was falling hard for this girl.

But I was also afraid that at the end of the summer she'd leave, just like Julie.

I'd be alone, again, and back in a spiral.

I couldn't get too close.

No matter how much I found myself falling just as hard for her.

"HEY, AIN'T THAT YOUR girl?" Rico called, as I removed the last of the orange cones that separated the new road from the old one.

I looked up and saw her blonde wavy hair before the two bags in her hand as she slowly approached the road barrier.

"Yeah, it is," I said, putting the last of the cones in the truck.

"Man, your little mama looks even hotter while pregnant. Think she'd be up for some brown wood?"

I smacked Rico on the back of the head. "In your fucking dreams, man."

I didn't look back at him as I sauntered up to the barrier. "Hey, baby, what are you doing here? I thought you had class?"

She smiled, biting down on her bottom lip. "I did, but I just had to turn in my final paper and I was done, so I thought I'd bring you lunch. You know, my version of hunting."

I rubbed the back of my neck. "Yeah...about this morning..."

She shook her head and put her hand up. "Let's not talk about that right now. Can you take a break and eat with me? I got burgers and fries from Sam's."

I stepped around the barrier and took her hand. "That sounds great."

I opened the tailgate of my Blazer and we sat on the back. Usually I brought my lunch, but having something hot was much better.

"How much bacon did you get on these things?" I asked.

Libby giggled. "I've been craving it, sorry!"

I pinched her arm with my free hand. "No, I like it. I like when you eat, it provides nourishment for our little William Robert."

She wrinkled her nose. "You know we vetoed that name once my sister pointed out that it could be shortened to Billy Bob."

"Okay...then what do you suggest?"

She swung her legs back and forth and shrugged. "I don't know. We don't need to decide that right now."

"Yes we do. We've both put it off long enough. You're right, baby. I've been ignoring you for what I want to do, we should decide."

She blinked slowly, staring at me. "Who are you and what have you done with my husband?"

I laughed. "I'm right here, baby. Come on. Throw some names out at me."

She shook her head. "No, seriously, I've been a real bitch. You've been working your butt off while I sit at home and eat bacon."

I grinned. "I like it when you sit at home and eat bacon."

"Maybe after the baby is here we can talk about me working more hours...maybe I can pick up another job...then you wouldn't have to work as hard."

I put my hand on hers. "Let's not talk about that now. Let's worry about that after he's here. Now tell me some of those names I know you've been thinking of."

She smiled before slowly pulling her phone out of her purse. "Well, I went through some baby name sites and found a few that I really liked."

"Okay. Lay them on me."

"We have...Noah, Cain, Daniel, Eli, Gabriel, Gideon..."

I grabbed her phone and looked at the list, which had to be at least fifty pages long. "Are these all bible names?"

She smiled. "Some. There are also celebrity baby names and some traditional Creole names."

I raised my eyebrows. "You want to give our baby a Creole name?"

She shrugged. "I figured it couldn't hurt to look."

I scrolled down the list. "Okay, some of these aren't too bad. I could probably live with an Abel or Andre, but not Baptiste."

She giggled. "Yeah, I was just adding some random ones in there."

"I think our boy needs a Creole name, but something traditional. Who knows, maybe someday he'll want to go to school in Chicago and marry a city girl."

"I don't know if little Gaston would want to go up north," Libby said.

I scrolled down the list again, stopping on one name that caught my attention. "Yeah, but Mathieu might."

Libby looked at the list. "Is that how it's pronounced? Like Matthew?"

I laughed. "How did you think it was?"

"Math-A-wee," she said, with an over-enunciated French accent.

I shook my head. "Naw, baby. It's like the traditional name and I like it. Mathieu Crabtree."

She smiled. "I like it too. A lot."

I glanced at her. "Did we just pick our baby's name?"

"I think we did."

I leaned in and kissed her gently.

"Hey, Crabtree, quit making out. Get back to work so we can head to Reesey's!" Jackson yelled and I cringed, pulling back to see Libby's wrinkled nose.

"What did he just say?"

I rubbed the back of my neck. "Well, Jackson and some of the guys were going to head to the pool hall after work today. The job's almost done and tomorrow will be a short day since it's the day before a holiday and they thought it'd be nice to celebrate a little. You know, unwind."

I was rambling and I knew it. She knew it too because the scowl on her face was pretty tight.

"And you weren't going to tell me? Just make me think you were working more overtime while you partied with your friends and I worked my ass off with swollen feet at my, you know, minimum wage job, as you called it."

"Baby, I was just upset when I said that, I didn't mean it," I said, keeping my voice low. The guys didn't need to hear us fighting; that would just add more fuel to the fire. They'd start yelling jabs and even after Libby left they'd give me shit.

"Obviously you did or you wouldn't have said it. Now, what, you're just going to go out with the guys and keep things from me? What else are you keeping from me?"

I winced and of course she caught it, folding her arms over her chest. "Seriously? Is there something else you need to tell me?"

I rubbed the back of my neck. "Well, I didn't want it to come out this way..."

She gritted her teeth. "Now it is, so just tell me."

"I got my assignment for my new job yesterday. It's the highway extension in New Orleans."

She blinked rapidly. "The one that's by the bridge?"

I nodded, swallowing hard. "Yeah. The foreman thinks it'll be a great opportunity for me to move up."

She nodded, looking down. "It probably is..."

"It's only an extra forty-five minutes to my commute and I'll make sure that I have all the time off I need when Mathieu is born. This could be great for us and our future."

I didn't know she was crying until she looked up and tears were streaking her cheeks. "You're going to be farther away from me. I barely get to see you now. When am I ever going to see you?"

I wrapped my arms around her and pulled her close, as she pressed her face to my chest and sobbed while I rubbed her back. "It's okay, baby. We'll make it work. It's going to all work out."

But even as I said the words, I wasn't even sure myself how anything was going to work.

Chapter 5

After work I decided to stop by the grocery store. Libby was working at Dee's shop until close and after our scuffle that afternoon, I decided to surprise her with dinner.

The local grocery store was small and overpriced, but it did well in a pinch and it was better than driving another thirty minutes to something larger and better. I also had a thing about shopping local and supporting Elsbury.

I was a simple man, though, and my cooking ability was pretty limited. Basically, I knew how to put stuff on the grill and pour out a bag of salad mix into a bowl.

I sauntered down the produce aisle, scanning for the mixed bags of salad. They had to be somewhere.

"Hey, Blaine."

I winced.

That voice. One I was all too familiar with. A voice that the last time I heard it, had been when she was drunk at my wedding.

I put my hands up and stepped forward. Nikki had way too much bourbon and I knew when that happened she either got super angry or super horny. By the way she stood with her hands clenched into tight fists, I knew it was the former. "Now, I think you've had a little too much to drink. Why don't I go find Bubba to take you home?"

She swatted my hands and scowled. "No! I'm speaking the truth! Do you really think you're going to be happy? You're just marrying her because she's knocked up and now you have to go home to her bitching every night. You'll never get to go out with your friends. This is the end of the line, Blaine Crabtree and I hope you're happy with it."

I turned slowly to see her standing next to the display of watermelon. She was wearing a red employee polo and khaki shorts, her blonde hair was pulled back into a ponytail and made her look more demure than the usual wild country girl I was used to.

We had a fling, I'll admit that. When Julie dumped me I made a lot of mistakes, and one of the big ones was jumping into bed with Nikki. I knew she'd always had a crush on me. Hell, she was Bubba's little sister who was always fishing or mudding with us. I never thought of her as an actual girl for the longest time, but she definitely was. And definitely the girl I didn't want to be around.

"I didn't know you worked here..."I said, my words trailing. If I would have known she did, I probably would have driven the extra thirty minutes.

"Yeah, Dad's business is kind of slow so I've been picking up a few shifts here stocking shelves."

I nodded. "That's cool. I mean, not about your daddy's shop being slow, but cool that you have another job."

She let out a deep breath then laughed. "Wow. This isn't awkward at all."

I shook my head. "It ain't awkward for me. I'm not the one who got drunk and made a scene at my wedding."

She scrunched her face as if I just slapped her then closed her eyes and sighed. "Yeah, I guess I deserve that. Sorry I fucked up and ruined your wedding."

"Nikki, you didn't ruin my wedding. Nothing could have. You know I'm with Libby, right? I'm going to stay with her. This isn't some fly by night relationship. I know I've been with a lot of other girls and hell, I know I probably hurt them in the process, including you, but this is different."

She shrugged. "If you say so."

"If you have something to say, Nikki, you can say it. I probably won't listen to it, but if I'm spitting some truth bombs, then you might as well fire back at me."

She shook her head. "It's just...you used to be carefree. Happy. You were always out with the guys, mudding, fishing, and hunting. Now you don't. You're always working or cooped up in your Meemaw's house doing God knows what. I just want you to be happy. Not because we had a fling, but because we're friends."

"I am happy," I said through gritted teeth.

I may have said the words, but I honestly wasn't sure. Yes, I loved Libby. Yes, I was happy that I married her. But I did miss my friends. I did miss going out without a care in the world. But I was older now. I had a family on the way. Those days were probably over forever.

She blew out a breath of air from between her teeth. "Well, if you're happy then I guess I'm happy for you."

"Good."

She clasped her hands together. "Now that that awkward conversation is over with, can I help you find something?"

I laughed. "Yeah, point me in the direction of the premade salads."

I HAD DINNER SET ON the table before Libby even came home. I had to admit that the fancy little gray bowls and serving dishes actually made the old farmhouse table look a tiny bit dressier.

I lit some candles and put them on either side of the tray of bacon wrapped filets that I picked up from the butcher. Aside from the bag of salad, I also picked up some bacon potato salad and bacon pork rinds, hoping that would satisfy her cravings. It also sounded disgusting, but they had a pint of maple bacon ice cream in the freezer section, so I threw that in the cart as well. I had to do something to apologize for my assholeishness.

The door creaked open and Libby's footfalls fell on the hard wooden floor before I heard her gasp as she entered the kitchen. "What is all of this?"

I put my arms around her waist and then pulled her toward the table. "Bacon feast for my favorite girl and little man."

"You cooked?" she raised her eyebrows.

I nodded. "Well, I grilled."

She giggled. "Yeah, I remember last time you tried to use the stove, you almost burnt down your mom's house."

"Hey! I'll learn! Eventually..."

"I should be the one cooking for you...hormonal, crazy, pregnant Libby kind of took over earlier."

I shook my head. "Naw, baby, you were only speaking the truth."

"No. I was out of line. You've been doing nothing but working long hours and taking care of me, you deserve some time with your friends. Hell, and if you want this job in the city, then do it. It'll be a great opportunity for all of us."

I raked my fingers through my hair. "I don't know. I may just tell the foreman it'd be better if I stayed around Elsbury."

She put her hand on my bicep. "Don't. If this is what you want to do, I'm going to support it. As long as you get the time off when Mathieu is born, I'll be here."

I raised an eyebrow. "Are you sure?"

She leaned in and lightly kissed my lips. "With you, Blaine, I'm always sure."

THE NEXT DAY OF WORK was our last day on the job, so we ended early with our paychecks in hand.

Jackson opened his envelope, then swatted me with it. "You know what this little bonus is going for? Imma get a new grill built for the back. Won't be in for the Fourth tomorrow, but you bet your ass it's going to be ready for Labor Day and every party after."

I forced a smile but it fell as soon as I looked at my paycheck. Before I would have been happy with it. Maybe used the extra money to buy something for my truck. But now I didn't have my truck and most of the money was going to go toward utilities and finishing the kitchen remodel. I didn't even know if there would be any left for furniture and what the hell Libby would say about it.

"Blaine, are you even listening to me?" Jackson asked.

"Yeah, sure, sounds great, man."

Jackson laughed. "You didn't hear a word I said."

"Yeah, I did."

"Then what did I say?"

I shook my head and let out a single laugh. "Okay, you got me. I didn't hear a damn thing you said."

"That's what I thought." He slapped my back. "I was asking if you and Libby were still going to come out to the house."

"Yeah. We just have to stop and see Britt play in her tournament game, then we'll be over."

"All right. Dina and I are looking forward to seeing you."

I just hoped it was better than our last Fourth of July. Libby wore a sexy lingerie set and I wanted to devour her in it. But not there. Not in Jackson's room. Not in the place where the beginning of my fall started.

Julie had been busy the first few weeks of school. Sorority rush and all that. I missed her something fierce, so I decided just to give in and drive the eight hours to Oxford.

I rolled up to her dorm with a box of her favorite things: my mama's homemade pralines, cherry cola, and licorice rope. It was cheesy, but I wanted something to bring a smile to her face.

I expected all dorms to look like the movies, but instead of being a place where everyone hung out in the hallways, it felt more like a prison.

She was in an all-girls dorm and I couldn't even get past the door without having a female escort me. That didn't stop me from sneaking in behind a group of girls in some Greek letter shirts when the front desk lady's back was turned.

I bounded up the stairs two at a time, to the second floor where Julie's room was. There wasn't a single soul walking the hallway and I wondered if there was some big mass exodus that I missed the memo on. Walking past a small kitchenette, I turned and saw her room number. There was a dry erase board on the door with the words 'Julie and Lisa's room' written across it in some girly handwriting. There was also a picture of Julie on one side of it and her roommate on the other.

Damn I had missed Julie's face. And other parts of her. I think I'd masturbated so much I was starting to chafe.

I knocked on the door and heard some rumbling from behind it, then hushed whispers.

At least she was home.

The door cracked open and Julie stared at me wide-eyed. She was in her bathrobe, which I thought it was kind of late in the day for, but I didn't know the college lifestyle. Maybe she was just getting around to showering.

"Blaine! What are you doing here?"

I smiled and held up the box. "I thought I'd come and surprise you with some of your favorites. Maybe I can even take you out for dinner."

She shook her head, keeping her hand firmly on the door between us. "Oh, no. Sorry, I have a thing with the Kappas tonight."

"A thing? I just drove eight hours, surely you could make some time for me. It's been awhile."

She looked behind her and then back at me. "I know, it has. I'm just really busy right now. I told you that the last time we talked."

Her eyes kept darting behind her and I knew something was up.

"Yeah? Busy with school or someone else?"

She scoffed. "Don't be silly."

Her eyes darted back again and I couldn't help it, I pushed on the door and she stepped backward, revealing her tiny dorm room. I didn't focus on the crimson bedspread that I helped her pick out or the football poster. I zeroed in on the guy standing next to it, trying desperately to get into his jeans.

"Blaine, this isn't what it looks like," she stammered.

"Really? Cuz what I'm seeing is a half-naked man in my girlfriend's room."

"You have a boyfriend?" the guy asked, his accent making him sound like a California surfer.

"Yeah and who the hell are you?" I asked, folding my arms over my chest and flexing.

"That's none of your concern, bro."

"Oh, I think it is," I said.

He laughed. "Well, then obviously I'm the guy fucking your girlfriend because your sorry Southern ass couldn't keep her satisfied."

As soon as he finished his sentence, Julie leaped forward, but it was too late because my fist already connected with the guy's jaw. He staggered backwards before lunging at me with his fists blazing.

We rolled around on the ground, punching and kicking as Julie screamed behind us.

There was a flurry of people that came in and finally broke us apart. I thought Julie might talk to me. Say something. Anything. But instead she went over to the other guy, tenderly rubbing his cheek then turned toward me, glaring.

"That was unnecessary, Blaine!"

"Seriously? I just caught you cheating on me and you're going to act like I'm the bad guy."

She rolled her eyes and stepped forward, grabbing my arm and leading me in the other direction. "Look, Blaine. We had some good times. But that was high school. This isn't going to work long distance. You and I both know that."

"So you're breaking up with me like this? You couldn't have done it before you cheated?"

She sighed. "I know. I should have. I should have the moment I left that damn God forsaken town and promised I'd never go back."

"Did I mean anything to you at all?" I shouldn't have asked it.

She sighed. "Yeah. You did. But that was the past and I think we both know that the head cheerleader and jock are a cliché that should stay in high school. We were never going to work."

I didn't even say goodbye. I just left and called Jackson on my way out.

"Hey, buddy, you done screwing Julie or just taking a break?"

I groaned. "She cheated on me. I'm coming home."

"Oh shit, really?"

I nodded, walking to my truck and opening the door. "Yeah and you'd better have something strong waiting for me."

I DROVE WITHOUT CARING. I was going at least thirty miles over the speed limit, but I had to get away.

I never thought I'd be that guy. I'd always had the best of everything: the best truck, the best throwing arm, and what I thought was the best girlfriend.

Now I was just another single sap with a stupid story to go with it.

By the time I rolled into Jackson's place it was dark, but the lights were on in his house with a full party in place.

I walked through the door to be greeted with a lighted joint and a full beer. I didn't smoke much, but I wanted to do anything to get out of my own head.

I didn't know how many beers I drank or how much I smoked. I didn't even know I was passed out until Dina nudged me. "Hey, do you want to go sleep in Jacksons' room?"

I mumbled some sort of response and she helped me to my feet and walked me down the hallway where I collapsed on his bed. "You're so nice, Dina. You would never cheat."

She smiled. "I try to be a nice girl. It's hard, but we all have our strengths."

I WOKE UP THE NEXT morning completely butt ass naked in Jackson's bed and not remembering a damn thing that happened.

Slowly I opened my eyes and then closed them again when the bright sunlight hit them.

"What. The. Fuck."

Jackson came barreling into the room. "Well, look who's finally up."

"Yeah, man, what the hell? Did someone rufie my drink? I thought that was only for chicks."

Jackson crossed his arms over his chest. "You're the one naked in my bed."

I looked down at where the blanket covered me. I still had a condom on. It wasn't full, but it was there. "Fuck. Man. What did I do?"

"Do you really not remember?"

I shook my head. "No. Please tell me I didn't hook up with some dude or get raped."

He sighed. "I found you in here with Dina."

"WHAT?" I sat straight up. "No, man, that can't be true. I was too lit to even get it up. There's no way I'd be with your woman."

"Well, that's what I fucking saw."

I stood up, making sure the blanket covered me. "Listen, man. After what I just went through with Julie, there is no way I'd fuck your girl. No way."

Jackson shook his head. "By your state, I'm guessing you didn't have much to do with it, but Dina...that's another story."

"I swear to you, brother, I wouldn't do that to you."

"I know I saw you both naked in my bed."

"And I swear that I don't know what happened, if anything. I'm so sorry."

Jackson stared out the window. "Well, sometimes sorry doesn't always cut it, does it?"

Chapter 6

Fourth of July was my first long weekend that I'd had off in a while. That meant that I'd get in a lot of time to work on the house.

"Are you going to spend all day putting up those shelves?" Libby asked, walking into the kitchen. Her hair was still wet from the shower and falling over her shoulders.

"Naw. I just want to finish this row before we head to the parade."

She nodded. "It's looking really good."

I stepped off the ladder and stood back, admiring the white shelves. "Yeah. They are, aren't they?"

"The gray tile really makes them pop. I can't wait until you and your dad get in the granite."

"Yeah, he's supposed to come in tomorrow."

She raised her eyebrow. "Then we can go furniture shopping?"

I rubbed the back of my neck. "Yeah...about that..."

"What? What now? Did you break something and we need to shell out more money for it?"

I shook my head and laughed, even though it wasn't funny in the least bit. "No, nothing's broken it's just...well...the paycheck wasn't as big as I thought it would be, but you know I'm sure we could find something nice maybe at the resale shop, or maybe my mom has something we could use."

She wrinkled her nose. "I don't want someone's used furniture."

I groaned. "Do you really need to be a snob? I don't know if you've noticed, but we aren't exactly made of money."

She scoffed. "I'm not a snob."

"Yeah, you kind of are and you know it."

"Well, excuse me for wanting nice things. I just don't see the point on spending money on something that's going to fall apart when we could get something nice that'll last forever."

"Yeah, but your idea of something nice is in the millionaire price range and we don't have that, baby. If you haven't noticed, we're just scraping by as it is."

She frowned. "We're not poor."

"No, but we ain't exactly rolling in it either. We just need to spend our money a little bit more wisely. I know that's hard for you to understand, but I'm sure we can budget for something."

"Because I'm a snob I wouldn't understand?"

I sighed. "Now, baby, I didn't say that."

"Look, I'll admit that I'm used to always getting what I want. I always have. And I knew that once I got pregnant and we decided to take the next steps together, that things were going to change. I accepted that. I lived with it, but it's hard. It's so freaking hard to roll with the punches." A sob escaped her lips and big tears fell down her cheeks.

I pulled her close and rubbed her back. Damn, these hormones were making her even more crazy than usual. "Shhh, it's okay, Lib. We're going to be all right. It may suck right now, but we're going to get through this."

"Some days I'm not sure we are," she cried.

I tucked my fingers under her chin and lifted her face so that her glossy eyes met mine. "What's that supposed to mean, baby?"

She sniffled. "I'm holding you back, I know it. You haven't touched your guitar or seen your friends since we've been married. All you've done is go to work, sleep, and work on this house. If I wasn't around, you'd still have your truck, your friends, and a girl that didn't cry at the drop of a hat." She burst into tears again and I pulled her close, running my fingers through her hair. "Libby, I don't want any other girl and

I'm happy. I really am. You and Mathieu are what matters most to me, okay? Whatever I have to do to make sure that we're all okay, I'll do it."

Her whole body shook as another sob escaped. "I don't want you to have to sacrifice anymore for me."

I held onto her shoulders and stepped back, leaning down and looking into her eyes. "Baby, I promise you that nothing is a sacrifice. I want all of this. I want our little family. You're all I've ever wanted."

"If you say so. I'm still not sure I believe it." She sniffled.

I leaned in and kissed her full on the lips. "Believe it."

FOURTH OF JULY IN A small town was always a big event. When I was in high school, it was the time I'd see all my friends I hadn't seen all summer and we'd check out the girls at the parade. Then we'd see if said girls would be willing to make out behind the Ferris wheel at the festivities that took place at the high school parking lot. Maybe even get to second base while watching the fireworks.

But not this year. Sure, we were still going to the parade but I didn't think there would be any making out behind the Ferris wheel, unless of course Libby was up for that. A little over the dress fondling couldn't hurt either of us.

"Did you bring any water bottles or anything?" Libby asked, sifting through the car.

"No, you didn't ask me to."

"Blaine! It's like a million degrees out. What if we die of poor hydration?"

I laughed, shaking my head. "I'm sure we can get something at the fair."

"Yeah, but they'll charge like five dollars for a bottle of water. Stop at the store real quick, then we can go to the shop."

"Libby..."

I glanced at the clock. The parade started at ten and it was already 9:40. Dee always had a place for us to park in back, but I knew traffic would be blocked soon and Libby would bitch if we had to walk a few blocks.

"Please? For Mathieu?"

I glanced at her out of the corner of my eye, where she was giving me big puppy dog eyes and rubbing her stomach.

I sighed. "Fine!"

"Yeah!" she squealed.

"How long are you going to keep using him as an excuse?"

She laughed. "As long as I can."

Usually the local grocer was pretty empty, but today the parking lot was packed. I did a quick scan, and didn't see Nikki's truck, which was lucky for small miracles. Hormonal Libby did not need a run in with her right now.

That didn't mean everyone else in town wasn't in the store.

"Blaine Crabtree, the best pitcher this town has ever seen!" I turned just as we walked through the door to see my old baseball coach, Rene Casteel, standing by the register. He walked over to me with a plastic bag in one hand and briskly shook my hand with the other.

Rene was always a big man. He had to be at least six foot five and was built like a moose. A gray, long-haired moose.

"I'm going to go grab the water bottles," Libby said, slinking past me.

Rene glanced behind me and then caught my eye as he let go of my hand. "I see you've been busy."

"Yeah, you know I'm an old married man now with a baby on the way. He'll be here in September."

Rene laughed, slapping his knee. "Well, I'll be damned. I never thought I'd see the day that happened. Is she a girl from Elsbury?"

I shook my head. "No, Libby's from Chicago. She's Dee Badeaux's niece."

"Ah, I see." He nodded, then patted my back. "Well, it was good running into you, boy. Hey, if you get a chance, stop over at the field today. I'm sure some of the boys playing in the tournament could use your eye."

I smiled. I probably wouldn't do it, but the thought was nice. "Thanks, Coach. Will do."

Before he was even a few steps away, I heard another small voice.

"Blaine, is that you?"

Every hair on my body stood on end. It was the last voice I ever wanted to hear or thought I would again.

I turned slowly to see a wide-eyed Julie staring back at me.

I hated to admit it, but she also looked amazing in a tight-fitting red tank top, short shorts, and her hair pulled back. I'd also be lying if I didn't say my eyes lingered over her low neckline. But I shook the thoughts of anything sexual out of my head. I was a married man and this was the girl that almost broke me.

"Hey, Julie, didn't expect to see you around here." I forced the biggest smile I could, but kept my distance. I wasn't going to hug her or shake her hand.

"Yeah. I actually have a summer internship on Magazine Street, so Dani said I had to come into town for the parade. Her daddy is driving the tractor in it, as usual, and she's afraid he may die of heat exhaustion," she said with her usual ramble when she got nervous. I never forgot her rambling. It was something I missed and hated at the same time.

"Yeah, didn't think you were ever going to come around these parts again."

Her face fell and she nodded. "Yeah. Sometimes things change."

"Blaine! They have bacon chocolate bars and they're on sale, so I got five!" Libby came bounding toward me with half a chocolate bar in her mouth.

She stopped and swallowed hard and looked between me and Julie. Julie's eyes widened even more as she stared at Libby's large stomach. "Oh, hello, Libby is it?"

Libby took a big bite of her chocolate bar and with a full mouth said, "You can call me Mrs. Crabtree."

"Oh. Yeah. Dani said something about you two getting married and I guess you're starting a family. Congrats." Julie put on her fake smile; the one she used that made her the pet of every teacher in school.

Libby looped her arm through mine. "Gee, Julie, I'd love to say it was nice to see you, but it's not. We have to go now. We'll probably be making out or something, hopefully we don't see you again, have a great day. Bye!" Libby pulled me through the door and out to the muggy air.

"Wow, that wasn't awkward at all," Libby said, chewing her chocolate bar as she got into the car.

"There wasn't a need to be rude," I mumbled, starting the car.

"Really? That was your ex-girlfriend. One of the biggest bitches I've ever met. I mean, not that you have a nice ex, but her and Nikki are pretty much cream of the crop."

I shook my head and let out a short laugh. "Yeah, like that douchebag, frat boy ex of yours is any better."

She finished the last of her chocolate bar and shoved the wrapper back in the bag. "Yeah, but he doesn't always show up and try to put a move on me."

"He probably would if he lived here."

"No. He's a stripper in Chicago."

I turned my head sharply toward her. "How do you know he's a stripper? Did he come give you a private dance at your bachelorette party or something?"

She laughed. "Actually, yes. The guy is so dumb he didn't put two and two together that it was my sister who hired his company. It was actually quite humorous."

I shook my head, clenching my hands on the steering wheel. "And you didn't think it would be a good idea to tell me that your ex was at your bachelorette party and getting naked for you?"

She rolled her eyes. "Seriously? It's a stripper. A male stripper. There is nothing sexy about some guy dancing and waving a dick in my face."

"It must have meant something if you felt the need to keep it from me."

"Oh my god, are you seriously getting jealous right now?"

I tightened my jaw. I didn't want to be. I'd only met her ex once and I decked him in the face after he called Libby a bitch. He was a stereotypical frat rat with spiky hair, sunglasses even at night, and wasted off his ass. I couldn't believe she didn't tell me he got naked at her bachelorette party.

"I'm not jealous. I just don't understand why you wouldn't tell me that." I tried to keep my voice even, but inside I was fuming. All of these months and she couldn't bother to tell me that she had recently seen her ex naked.

"Because it was stupid. Yes, my ex is now a stripper and my husband is a hard-working man and way better at everything. Obviously I did a better job and married up."

I didn't say anything and she put her hand on my cheek, turning my face toward hers. "Look, Blaine Crabtree, I may be hormonal. I may be crazy, but I'm also crazy about you and I'd like to think you're just as crazy about me. So to make both of us happy and not get even crazier, can we just agree to stop with the jealousy shit and get to Aunt Dee's? We've probably already missed the fire trucks and I'd really like some candy."

I didn't want to stop the conversation, but there was really nothing else to say. If we kept talking, then we'd just keep arguing. So I nodded and then kissed her cheek before slowly backing out of the spot.

"So...who was that older guy you were talking to?"

"That was my high school baseball coach and he wants me to stop by the tournament later today. We don't have to, but it might be nice."

I glanced at Libby out of the corner of my eye, expecting her to wrinkle her nose or roll her eyes, but instead she smiled. "I think that's a great idea."

I turned toward her, then looked back at the road. "Seriously?"

"Yeah, why not? You love baseball and you haven't played in a while. It couldn't hurt to maybe stop by since we have to see Britt play anyway."

I put my hand on hers on the console between us and squeezed her hand. "Awesome. Thanks, baby."

"No need to thank me. It's just what wives do. When I know something makes you happy and it doesn't hurt us, then I'm going to push you to do it. I don't want you to end up hating me."

"I could never hate you, Libby."

She sighed. "You say that now, but when Mathieu is born and we're both without sleep and you just want to get away, you may not be saying that."

I pulled her hand to my mouth and brushed my lips against her knuckles. "Never."

AFTER THE PARADE, LIBBY and I walked hand in hand down the small downtown area to the high school where the boys were already warming up on the field.

Coach was standing near a boy on the pitcher's mound, his head down. He re-arranged his cap backwards and forward on his head while the boy starred at him wide-eyed. It was a familiar look for Coach, the same thing he always did when he was pissed at the way I was throwing.

I approached the dugout and leaned on the fence, grabbing the metal. A couple of the guys were standing around, watching the field.

"Hey, what's going on out there?" I asked, nodding toward the mound.

One of the guys glanced back at me, then pointed at the scared looking kid standing by Coach. "Brady's throwing for shit again at practice. He gets hot, then gets cocky, and it fucks the rest of us up."

I smiled, shaking my head. "Yeah, I know how that goes."

Coach would get on my ass all the time for getting cocky when I was in high school. He was the first person to really keep me in check, until Libby came around.

I glanced at her out of the corner of my eye. Maybe having someone around like that wasn't always a bad thing. I hated it in high school, but seeing it from the other side, started to make sense. It may seem like they're riding your ass, but really they're making sure you don't fuck up.

Coach looked toward the dugout, scanning it before his eyes locked mine and he motioned for me to come forward. I pointed at myself and looked around. Surely he didn't want me to go out there?

Coach nodded and signaled me again.

"Wait here one sec, baby," I said to Libby and then jogged out to the mound.

"What's up, Coach?" I asked, standing next to him and trying to block the sun. It was dead center on the mound and I don't know how the pitcher was managing without wearing sunglasses, his hat couldn't have even been fully covering him.

Coach put his hand on my shoulder. "Brady, this is Blaine Crabtree, the best pitcher Elsbury has ever seen. He'll tell you that you're getting too damn cocky and when you get cocky, you throw for shit."

"Am I supposed to just repeat exactly what you said?" I asked.

Brady laughed, then stopped when Coach gave him a stern look. "Not everyone can be an ace, son, but if you keep throwing brushbacks, I'm going to call in Frankie to take your place."

Brady nodded. "I know, sir. I know."

Coach patted my back. "Have a talk with him, son. I'm going to go grab a Gatorade."

I watched Coach jog toward the dugout, then turned to Brady. "You know, he may be a hard ass, but he knows what he's talking about."

Brady shook his head. "Yeah, I know. I'm just a little rusty. Haven't played since the spring."

"Is that your problem, or is it because you forgot your sunglasses at home and you're too embarrassed to call your mom to bring them for you? I figure it's either that or you're waiting to get out of here to get laid by the little brunette in the stands who keeps giving you fuck-me-eyes. Maybe it's a combination of both?"

Brady looked past me at the bleachers, where sure enough the little brunette waved at him and he nodded at her before looking back at me. "Okay, so maybe I'm not really into the game right now. I mean, come on, it's the fucking Fourth. What does it matter? It's not a real game."

"What matters is that Coach looks at this game as his set up for the rest of the year. If you keep getting in a jam now, he's going to look at that for the next season and maybe call on one of the guys from the bench to come in."

I put my hand on his shoulder and faced toward the bleachers, nodding toward the girl. "I know you don't want your girl to see you ride the bench all season, but don't get too cocky either. Find your sweet spot and settle in, then keep it there. Trust your catcher more than you trust your fucking girlfriend. If you stay in the zone and stop focusing on everything else, then you'll keep your spot as starting pitcher. I guarantee it."

He nodded. "Thanks, Crabtree. I appreciate it."

I smiled, patting his shoulder. "And go see if you can borrow your girlfriend's sunglasses too."

He laughed. "Yeah, I'll do that or see if one of the guys can loan me a pair."

I nodded. "All right, man, good luck."

I jogged back out to the fence, where Coach was standing next to Libby with his arms folded over his chest. "It's like I said, Libby, he's a natural."

I turned over my shoulder to see Brady throw a pitch that was high and tight, much better than the bush leagues he was throwing when I first came up.

I shrugged and turned back to Coach and Libby. "He just needed a little pick-me-up."

"Yeah, and that pick me up could go a long way with our JV team that's hiring an assistant coach," Coach said.

"Are you trying to say...?"

Coach smiled and patted my shoulder. "Give me a call at the athletic department office on Monday, Blaine. I'll need to call you in for an interview, but it's just a formality."

I rubbed the back of my neck. "I don't know, Coach. Work is awfully busy and I'm not really qualified. I don't have a degree or nothing."

"Son, you're more than qualified. You know the game better than half the dumb fucks who walk into my office asking for the job."

"I think you should do it, Blaine," Libby piped up.

I raised my eyebrows at her and she bit down on her bottom lip. "It wouldn't be until the spring, so we'll have plenty of time to get things figured out. Just go for it."

I'd thought about getting back into baseball for so long, but never thought of myself as a coach. Just having the two of them believe in me, meant a hell of a lot though.

"All right, Coach. I'll give you a call."

It was the biggest game of the season.

The biggest game of my career in high school baseball.

I should have been hyped up. I should have been giving my all and going in hot while the Ole Miss recruiter was watching.

But I choked.

More than once.

It took Coach until the bottom of the fourth before he finally approached the mound and I knew my time was up.

Lawrence LeBaron, the hotshot freshman, was already warming up to relieve me.

Coach stepped up to the mound, looking down at the ground and shaking his head. "I don't need to tell you that you're playing like shit, Crabtree. Getting too hot?"

"Yeah, sir. Sorry."

Coach smirked. "I'm thinking it's less about you being hot and more about you hoping that you'll stay out of the eye of the recruiter sitting behind your little girlfriend."

I shook my head fiercely. "No, Coach. I'm just too cocky. Go on and take me out and let Lawrence bring it home for the win."

Coach put his hand on my shoulder. "Blaine, I've been coaching you for the past three years. I know when you're playing hot, when you're on a streak, and when you're throwing the game. This is throwing the game."

"I'm sorry, Coach. I don't want to fuck up this game and ruin our chance for the play offs."

"Look, I'm not pulling you off the mound. You're the best we have and you know it."

"Not right now," I muttered.

Coach glanced back at the dugout, then lifted his hat and turned toward me. "You aren't going to win me this game because you want to impress a recruiter or get laid by your cheerleader girlfriend. You're going to win this game because you're Blaine Crabtree; one of the best kids that's ever walked onto this field. You play with heart. You're fiercely loyal and honorable and I would trust you with anything, so I'm trusting you with this game for your team. Think you can do that?"

I swallowed hard before nodding. "Yeah, coach, I can do that."

CAIMON DIDN'T HIT A single ball the rest of the game. By the time the lights went on the field, I was already jogging off the mound and wiping the sweat that was caked on my brow.

Before I could reach for my water bottle, Julie was jumping into my arms and knocked it out of my reach.

"That was awesome, Blaine! I was sitting right in front of the Ole Miss recruiter and I know he was impressed! He's probably going to offer you a spot right here and now!"

I forced the biggest smile I could. "Yeah. I don't know if it works that way but it would be awesome."

"Blaine Crabtree?" A deep Southern accent asked.

Julie turned toward the guy with the baseball cap low over his eyes, then looked at me mouthing 'the recruiter'. "Call me when you leave, Blaine."

She beamed at the recruiter before she swayed away.

The guy moved forward and shook my hand. "Tom Slandry, Ole Miss."

I nodded. "Hello, sir, it's good to meet you."

"You played one hell of a game, son. I was worried there in the beginning, but you proved to be every bit the stud your coach said you would be."

"Thank you, sir."

This could have been my time to get cocky and brag that I was a shoe-in for all-parish as a junior but I just kept my mouth shut.

"I see you haven't committed anywhere yet. Are you waiting until your senior year begins or are there other schools I should know about?"

I shook my head. "No other schools, sir. I'm committed to working for the parish highway and roads department."

The last words flew out if my mouth before I could take them back.

Tom's eyes widened. "The road crew?"

I swallowed hard. "Yes, sir."

"You know the road crew will still be there after school; that is, if the majors don't call."

"I know, sir." I sighed, mustering up the courage to do what could be one of the biggest mistakes of my life.

"I'm a small town boy. Always have been. Always will be. I like playing the game but it isn't my life. I know if I play in college, it'll take the joy out of it and it'll become my life. I'd rather keep it fun. Something I actually enjoy, rather than a job."

Tom smiled, breaking his professional demeanor. "Well, that's not what I was expecting to hear when I approached you, but I can respect that."

He reached into his pocket and pulled out a card. "But keep me in mind if the small town boy decides to take a trip to Oxford."

I took the card knowing full well I'd never use it. Hell, I was surprise he still offered. "Thank you, sir."

Chapter 7

When we pulled up to Jackson's house, the smell of smoke from the grill wafted in the air. That, and fireworks were already going off in the back.

He and Dina had a shack that was a few miles from our house, but he really bought it for the land. All ten acres of it that backed up to a creek.

"I'm going to be the only one not drinking here and scarfing down bacon chocolate bars," Libby muttered, taking a bite of her third candy bar.

I put my arm around her and kissed her forehead as we walked up to the house. "Naw, I'm sure it'll be pretty tame."

She raised an eyebrow. "Is it ever tame here?"

I laughed. "Hey, they try sometimes."

She looped her arm around my waist. "You know, I did mean it about you applying for the assistant coach job."

"I didn't say that you didn't."

She looked up at me. Libby was tall for a girl. If she wore heels we were basically the same height. It was intimidating as hell at first, but as long as she was barefoot, and kept those long legs in my view, I was okay with it. "Blaine, I'm serious. If you want to work on the road crew forever like Jackson and your dad, that's fine. But if you want to do something else, something I know you really enjoy, then you should do it."

"But what about you? Hell, Libby, we've got a shit ton going on in our lives."

She smiled. "I'll be done with school in a few years and if you want to go back and get a coaching certificate or even a teaching degree, then

I'll support it. I'll get a better job in New Orleans and we can apply for every student loan out there."

I hadn't even thought that far ahead. My life was always planned out for me: play baseball in high school, start working on the road crew after I graduated, get married, retire at sixty. I never thought about veering off that plan. Hell, I had recruiters for college ball and I didn't even give them a second look. But maybe now it was time. Maybe having someone that pushed me for it meant something.

"Yeah, I think maybe we can talk about doing that. Let's take one step at a time and see if I get the job first."

She leaned in and kissed me hard on the mouth. "You will."

I pulled her closer, my fingers trailing down to her waist as I wrapped my arms around her. "When did you get so sure of yourself?"

She pressed her body against mine and instantly my dick responded, stiffening against her. "I don't know. Maybe it was watching you out there on the field. You're kind of a natural at everything. Baseball. Guitar. It's like you have magic hands."

I moved my hands down to her butt, cupping it lightly. "Yeah?"

"Get a room you two! We don't need to see y'all making another baby!" Butch Sinclair yelled from around the corner.

I let go of Libby and turned to see him standing there, his pale ass wearing nothing but a pair of plaid shorts. The Confederate flag tattoo on his chest was on full display as he chugged a beer.

"Yeah, yeah, don't get too jealous, Butch." I put my arm back around Libby and guided her around the house.

"Hey, if your girl ever gets tired of you, I'm sure I could get down with a pregnant woman." He laughed, which showed that he wasn't exactly playing with all of his teeth.

"In your dreams, Sinclair," Libby said, tossing her hair over her shoulder.

I grinned at Butch's shocked expression as we rounded the corner to the packed backyard. People stood around the cement patio where

Jackson had recently built a tin roof to help block out some of the Louisiana sun. Spanish moss trees did the rest of the work, lining almost the entire yard that led up to the creek. Dina stood behind a makeshift pallet bar that was set up between two trees and waved Libby over.

"Mind if I leave you for a while? I'm sure that Dina is hiding the good snacks back there for me." Libby raised her eyebrows.

I laughed. "Yeah, go ahead."

I watched her practically skip over to the bar where sure enough, Dina produced a small plate from behind it.

"Hey, Crabtree, got a minute?" a low voice asked.

I spun around to see Jackson standing there. The man was always in flannel, but today he was sporting a tank top that read "Star Spangle Hammered" and revealed just how pasty and freckle-covered he was.

"Yeah, man. Everything okay?"

He smiled. "I hope so."

I followed him past the crowd. He opened the screen door to the back porch and I followed him into the kitchen. Dina and he had definitely done some work to the former outdated, green kitchen. It was now completely open with white cabinets, gray granite countertops, and wooden floors.

"Man, y'all have definitely done some work. It feels like forever since I've been here," I said, looking around at the kitchen.

There used to be a paneled wall that separated it from the tiny living room that was mostly taken over by a big screen TV. But now the wall was knocked down and replaced with a breakfast bar that opened up to the living room with new beige colored walls, leather sofas, and a TV mounted above the fireplace where a moose head used to be.

Jackson looked over the room wistfully. "Yeah, Dina really helped me make this place a home."

I patted him on the back. "I'm really glad you two worked everything out, man. You seem really happy with her."

"I am. I really am."

I raised an eyebrow. "So why are you looking all like you just kicked in the nuts? Don't tell me you're about to break up with her."

He laughed, shaking his head as he leaned against the counter. "No, actually quite the opposite. I think I'm going to ask her to marry me."

I beamed and smacked him on the back again. "Holy shit, that's great news, man! Now I won't be the only married guy on the crew!"

He shook his head. "That ain't why I'm doing it."

"I know, I know. I was just saying."

He looked out the back door. "We've been together for a while and I planned on proposing that night I found you two..."

I rubbed the back of my neck. "Jacks, you don't know how sorry I am about that."

He put his hand up. "I know. You two were both wasted and, hell, you don't remember it. That's why I broke up with her, because I felt betrayed. But then it kind of made me look back at myself and wonder what the hell I was doing that made my girl jump in bed with my best friend, though she told me you passed out and she didn't get much past the tip from you. Worst lay ever."

I shoved his arm. "Hey!"

He laughed. "I have to find some humor in it."

"Fine, I'll give you that."

"Anyway, it took me a while, but I realized that I was being a shitty boyfriend, so when we finally did get back together, I knew I needed to tend to her needs as well as mine. At first it sucked because I tried doing all her girly shit and hated it, but then we found a common ground. We redid all of this together and now we're moving on to refinishing furniture. We're actually getting pretty good at it, thinking of selling some at Dee's shop."

"That's awesome, man. Good for you two."

He nodded. "The reason why I brought any of that up is because I know I give you a lot of shit about Libby. Hell, the whole crew does."

I shook my head. "Naw, I understand. I'm not getting sore over it. It's just what y'all do."

"Yeah, still, Blaine. You and Libby do have something special. Don't treat her like she's a burden. Once that baby comes around, I'm sure your life will get even crazier, but Dina and I will be here for you. Then maybe in a year, if Dina says yes, you'll be standing beside me as my best man and that little boy of yours will be the ring bearer."

I smiled. "Yeah, I think I'd like that."

"Well, all right." Jackson smacked my back.

I thought on his words as my eyes drifted over to the back porch where Libby stood, eating something off of a small red plate.

I'd spent so long thinking of all the shit I was missing by being with Libby, I was starting to forget the good things about her. Of course, I wasn't exactly the best at seeing things. It's why it took me so long to realize she had any problems at all. I thought she was just insecure, like girls can be. I didn't realize that there was anything wrong with her until I thought I lost her.

"I'm so excited, I'm so excited." Abby skipped into the room and plopped herself down on her mom's lap. The girl was always excited, running around in her little tutu. But this Thanksgiving she seemed like she was about to burst at the seams.

"What are you so excited for, baby?" Meg asked.

"Because Uncle Blaine and Aunt Libby are getting married, and I'm going to be the flower girl," she said matter-of-factly.

I blinked rapidly and starred at my little niece. She would always ask me when I was going to marry Libby and I just ignored her. I'd only been with the girl a few months, and while I loved her, and had been through a hell of a lot with her, I wasn't exactly ready for that commitment.

"Yer gettin hitched, Blaine, and you didn't even bother to tell me? Guess I better croak soon so y'all can have a house, and you aren't livin' with yer mama." Meemaw cackled.

I wasn't exactly sure what Meemaw even thought of Libby. She had poked her and called her a Yankee when she first met her. If that didn't embarrass me enough, now I had to deal with a tutued girl telling everyone I was getting hitched.

I shook my head, waving my arms in front of my face. "No, Meemaw. We aren't getting married."

I glanced at Libby who stared at me with wide eyes as if I just kicked her in the baby maker. Shit. Now I had to say something to make up for it. "I mean anytime soon. Not now. I mean…I don't know where Abby got that idea."

Meg laughed. "Abby, did someone tell you Blaine and Libby were getting married?"

Abby jumped off her mother's lap. "I thought it was about time that they did, so I decided they should."

Everyone at the table laughed. Thank God they found it funny. But when my eyes landed on Libby, she wasn't laughing. Her hand was on her head and she was blinking rapidly. She stood up from the table, her hand shaking as she gripped the chair. She moved her hand from the chair to the table, her hand swiping one of Mom's china plates. I couldn't move fast enough and it fell, shattering on the wooden floor below.

"Libby, are you okay?" I stood up, trying to reach for her arm, but she moved forward, toward the hallway.

"Libby!" I ran over to her and grabbed her wrist, spinning her around to me. Her eyes rolled back into her head and she collapsed in my arms.

"Ma! Dee! Someone call 9-1-1!" I yelled and cradled her close to me as I sat down on the ground, pushing her hair out of her eyes.

"Libby, baby, wake up."

She moaned and her eyelids fluttered slightly, but she didn't open them.

The sirens came closer and a flurry of activity started as the EMTs wheeled the gurney into the house. I didn't want to let her go. I couldn't.

"Sir, we're going to lift her up now."

I stared at the man, who looked at me expectantly. It took everything I had to let Libby go and hand her over as he took her limp body and put her on the stretcher.

"I'm going with," I yelled, following the stretcher.

Dee said something about calling Libby's parents and my mom yelled something, but I wasn't paying attention. All I could focus on was Libby's closed eyes and the fear that I was going to lose her.

THE HOSPITAL WAS THE most unwelcoming place in the world with horribly uncomfortable guest chairs. I sat watching Libby as the monitors blinked next to her.

Bulimic.

Libby had an eating disorder and I didn't even know it.

I always thought it was something that cheerleaders had, but never thought of it as real.

Not until I watched the person I loved most in the entire world crumble in my arms.

The doctors kept feeding her IV bags. Some had fluid and some had medicine. I didn't understand much of their medical talk, but I knew that things were bad.

That I almost watched my girlfriend die.

After everything we'd been through. All our fights. All the heartache and I didn't notice.

I didn't pay attention when she wouldn't eat at restaurants. The way she was always staring at her own body with disgust, even when her pants were practically falling off her hips.

I didn't tell her she was beautiful every single day like I should have.

Her mom would be coming in soon. Aunt Dee called her and the woman said she'd be on the first flight there. Until then, I wasn't leaving Libby's bedside and maybe not afterward either.

I'll admit, I didn't understand it all. I didn't understand why this beautiful girl just went without eating and why she couldn't just snap out of it.

It was something that I couldn't comprehend any of.

But as I watched her, laying there, immobile, I knew that I was going to have to learn. I was going to have to get over what would hold me back from helping her and just love her no matter what.

Chapter 8

My dad didn't know the meaning of a hangover. Not that I drank that much at Jackson's, but it would have been nice if I could have tried to sleep in a little and not have Dad knocking on the door at the ass crack of dawn the next morning.

I answered the door in just my boxers, still trying to rub the sleep from my eyes.

Dad stood there in his usual flannel button down and jeans, an LSU baseball cap low over his eyes. "What the hell are you doing answering the door like that, Blaine? What if I was someone coming to rob you and you were left defenseless in your underwear?"

Dad stepped around me and I shut the door behind him. "Well, my shot gun is in the closet over here and I'm pretty sure that if someone was trying to rob us, they wouldn't use the doorbell."

He nodded and kept walking down the hall, glancing in each room. "Looks like you've already done some work in here."

I shrugged. "Not too much. Just some paint and knocked down the cabinetsch in the kitchen. I need you for the bigger projects."

Dad stopped in the kitchen, putting his hands on his hips as he surveyed the room. I imagined this is what he did on road work projects too. He was made a foreman right after I was born, I didn't even know for sure if he remembered how to do manual labor.

"I hope you measured right, son, because this granite wasn't cheap."

"I know, I know. I promise I'll pay you back every dime. I just got paid and we've been running through it like it's water on an August day."

Dad laughed, shaking his head before putting his hand on my shoulder. "I'm not worried about it, son. Now get some clothes on so we can get to work."

I didn't know exactly what he meant about not worrying about it. There was no way in hell I was going to let him and Mom pay for the granite. They had their own shit that needed to be done at their place. I wasn't the type of guy to take handouts and I intended to pay every bit back.

EVEN THOUGH ALL THE upper cabinets were removed, there was still the business of taking out all of the appliances and cutting and fitting the plywood support.

I needed Dad for all of those things. If I could have done it myself, hell, I would have. But I didn't have half of the tools he did, and he was better at it than me.

"You sure you got those measurements right?" Dad asked for about the hundredth time as he set up the saw horses and laid down the first piece of plywood.

"I told you, I measured them almost every day, just to see if there was any change and make sure I got them absolutely correct."

He laughed. "Well, they're a lot bigger than I thought they were. Meemaw didn't do as much cooking when we moved out, so I'm guessing all that counter space was just for holding her cigarettes and Coke."

"Hopefully that's not all these will be used for. Too nice for that," I said, setting up the saw.

"You know, I noticed that there's still a lot of work you need to do in the living room and y'all haven't even touched some of the other rooms," Dad said as he put on his safety goggles.

My shoulders tightened. I didn't want to have this conversation with him. I didn't want him to think his only son couldn't handle the work.

"I've got it. We're going to live in this house for the rest of our lives. We've got time."

He shook his head. "But not much more time until the baby's here. You know, if you wanted to see about getting some of the work hired out, I've got some guys on my crew in Caimon who are always looking for side jobs. They're a real respectable bunch. They even did the remodel of the church hall out there and they do beautiful work."

So he really didn't think I could do it. Typical. Sounded just like Libby's dad.

Lunch at one of those frou frou places left much to be desired. My stomach was still grumbling and I was hoping that I could convince Libby to go on a walk with me and get a hot dog or something from a vendor. She was a few months pregnant and eating at least a little bit more. Maybe if we did that, then I could get away from her parents' death stares as well.

"Libby, Jack, do you mind if Libby and I had some girl time? We thought we would check out a dress shop off Wacker," Libby's mom said, looking at us with those big doe eyes.

I was sure she used that same face with her lips slightly parted, looking wide-eyed to make people in the courtroom think she was just another caring mom. That would be before she probably crushed their dreams in an instant.

"Sure, Kathryn, that'll give Blaine and I a chance to talk," Jack said, putting his hand on my back.

I tried not to cringe. The last conversation I had with the man was less than pleasant and I didn't want another one.

Libby waved out of the passenger side of the car, smiling like we didn't have a care in the world.

She didn't have to sit with her dad all afternoon.

Jack and I were both silent all the way up the elevator and through the front door of their lavish condo. Seriously, when I thought about condos it was always about those rinky dink places in Florida that old people stayed in during the winter. My grandma on my mom's side had one that we stayed in one summer. It smelled like moth balls and was always freezing.

Libby's parents' place was just the opposite. It was at least 3000 square feet with top of the line everything from wooden floors to the best appliances and floor-to-ceiling windows that looked out over Chicago. Everything about the place exuded luxury and I was just the poor peasant they let invade.

And now they were stuck with me.

"Have a seat, Blaine," Jack said, pointing toward the leather sectional where he took the seat across from where he was pointing.

Reluctantly I sat down, wishing I could be anywhere but there. I thought maybe I could fake being sick, and asked to lie down, but that wouldn't have gone over well either.

"So, Libby has told me that you work on the road crew in Elsbury."

I nodded. "Yes, sir. I've been doing that a few years now. I hope someday to make foreman."

That wasn't exactly true. I didn't actually know if I wanted to be a foreman, but at least it sounded good.

Jack nodded, crossing his arms over his chest. If he were my dentist, he would scare the shit out of me. He had a very tight jaw that he clenched every time he was pissed off.

"Do you plan on going to college? Any kind of school?"

I swallowed hard, then licked my lips before shaking my head. "No, sir. Not at this point. I wasn't much for academics in high school, more about sports, and I'm better working with my hands than sitting at a desk."

I winced, thinking I shouldn't have said that last part. Obviously I was good with my hands and other parts. That's precisely how I got his daughter pregnant.

"I have nothing against someone who does manual labor. My old man used to always say 'you can dig ditches or be CEO of a company as long as you're happy', but that also doesn't say much, since my old man is still one of the most successful dentists in the Chicagoland area."

"Heh...yeah."

I rubbed the back of my neck. Shit. What the hell was I supposed to say? I'd barely said two words to this man the entire time I'd known him and now I was stuck with him.

"I think LSU might be playing, do you want me to turn on the game?" Jack asked, grabbing one of the million remotes on the couch.

"Yeah. That'd be great." I let out a deep breath I didn't know I was holding in as the little gray French bulldog, Sally jumped on my lap.

"Sally, come here girl," Jack called her.

But she didn't move. Instead, she just curled up and buried her head against my stomach.

"I guess all my girls are leaving me for some Southern charm," Jack joked, but smirked.

"I'm sure I'm just someone new and she can smell my parents' dogs on me," I said, scratching Sally behind her ears.

"You're still living with your parents?" Jack raised his eyebrows.

He had already turned the game on, so I tried to keep my focus on the giant TV instead of him.

"For now, sir. Libby and I are looking for a place to rent."

He crossed his arms over his chest. "Why aren't you buying? You've been working for your company for a while. You should have good credit."

"I'm set to inherit my Meemaw's house in Elsbury. It's morbid, but I figured she was heading for a nursing home or the grave sooner rather than later, so I kind of always just waited around for that."

Jack nodded. "So that means you do have some money saved up?"

I winced. "Some, yes."

Okay, that was a lie. I had very little saved up. Most of my money went into my truck. I added a lift kit to it right before we found out Libby was pregnant, but I was never going to let her dad know.

Jack steepled his fingers. "Look, Blaine, I'm going to cut to the chase. I know you don't have a lot of money and that Libby is used to a certain lifestyle. She may act like she's happy right now, but it's only a matter of time before she's probably craving Tiffany's rather than bacon. Kathryn wanted me to suggest that we offer you a loan, no questions asked, no need to pay it back anytime."

I rubbed the back of my neck, searching for the right reply. The man basically just talked down to me like I was some poor little redneck. I didn't need his handouts, nor did I want them, but I had to play nice.

"Thank you sir, we appreciate your kindness, but I think we're good for now."

By the time we had the plywood base cut and screwed in, Libby had finally crawled out of bed.

I would have complained, but when I took one look at her wet blonde hair falling over her sun-kissed shoulders, I couldn't help but smile.

"Look who's finally up!" Dad said, enveloping Libby in a big hug. He always had a soft spot for the "Yankee Princess" as he called her.

"Yeah and since it looks like I'm not getting into the kitchen, do you want me to run into town and grab breakfast?"

I couldn't help but smile. It was good that she was remembering to eat. On more than one occasion I'd noticed she'd forgotten to eat dinner so I'd suggest late night pizza or a run to Sam's Drive-Thru. She never turned it down.

"Yeah, that sounds great, baby." I leaned over and kissed her forehead.

She wrinkled her nose and wiped a slick streak from her forehead. "You are one sweaty beast."

I picked up the corner of her tank top and wiped my face. She squealed and pulled back, giggling. "Oh my god! That's so gross!"

"You know you like it!" I pulled her close, wrapping my arms around her waist.

She squirmed against me. "Ew, no. You're so sweaty. I feel like I'm taking a sticky shower."

I gave her another quick kiss on her forehead, then let her go. "All right, all right. You win. Go get me a root beer and a breakfast burger. Once we get this granite in, I can maybe take a shower."

She laughed. "Yeah, you definitely need it."

She grabbed her keys from the hook near the fridge and headed out the front door.

I turned back to the counter and no sooner had I screwed in another nail was Libby yelling over the sound of the electric drill.

I whirled around to see her standing there with a big smile on her face.

"Back so soon?"

"Yeah, the UPS guy is here with a big delivery and I can't carry it."

I raised an eyebrow. I wasn't expecting anything else to come in for the remodel, but there could have been something I missed.

The brown truck was backed up to the house and the guy lifted up the back. I think his name was Steve or maybe Dave. He was a few years older than me in school and even at his age, he still had a face like a cherub.

"Hey, Blaine, got a big order here."

I wiped my face and hopped off the porch. "All right, man, I'll help you out."

He got in the back of the truck and pushed a large rectangular box forward. "This is the first one. It's a bit awkward and heavy as all get out."

"Okay." I held onto the back of it and pulled as he pushed it out before he jumped off the tailgate and we shuffled it to the front porch. This was followed by six more boxes.

"Damn, Blaine, what are y'all doing to the house?" Steve, or whatever, asked as we set the last box on the porch.

I shrugged. "A lot. I'm just not sure what this is."

"Must be pretty fancy if it's from Pottery Barn," Steve said, whistling through his teeth.

Libby's ears perked up and she examined the packages. "Pottery Barn? Did you order me furniture and not tell me?"

I shook my head. "I wish I could say I did."

"Well, I'll let you two lovebirds sort this out. Have a good day!" Steve, or whatever, said before he was off.

"Do you have your pocket knife on you?" Libby asked.

"Uh, yeah, always do." I brandished it from my pocket and she took it, slicing open the first of many packages.

There were a bunch of pieces of white wood with a note on top of it. Libby picked up the note and scanned it before covering her mouth. "Holy shit."

"What? What is it?" I asked, scooting closer to her.

"It's from my mom. She bought us all the furniture for Mathieu's room."

"No shit?" I stared at the paper and read the note.

Sorry we couldn't make your baby shower. Hopefully this set will make up for it.

Love you,

Mom and Dad

I was speechless. I didn't know if it was a compliment and something they were doing for their baby girl, or if it was just another dig at me. That I couldn't afford the nice things for her.

Libby squealed, reading over the paper. "It's the entire Gemma campaign! Crib, changing table, nightstand, and dresser! Oh the wingback rocker and the bedding with the little alligators printed on it and curtains to go with them! This is awesome! One last thing we have to buy! Can you and your dad put it together once you're done with the countertops?"

She stared up at me, the biggest smile on her face that I'd ever seen.

I wanted to ask why she was so happy when just a few months ago she was telling them that we wanted to do this all on her own. Why considering it a "gift" made any difference. But seeing her so happy, shut all that down.

"Yeah, baby, I'm sure Dad and I could do that."

DAD AND I DIDN'T GET done with the countertops until after lunch. The furniture in the baby's room didn't take as long as I thought it would, but still was one hell of a job.

Dad and I stood in the doorway with Libby in the middle of the room. She twirled around, flitting from the white crib to the large dresser and changing table, then sat on the wingback rocker for a few beats before jumping up again and running her fingers over the blanket with the tiny alligators printed on it that read "Mathieu" in blue stitched letters.

"This is beautiful. Thank you guys so much for putting it together," she said, turning toward us with tears in her eyes.

"Think nothing of it, darlin'. I'm just happy to be here to help," Dad said, embracing her in a big hug.

"But I'd better get going. Your Ma's probably wondering where the hell I am."

"Are you sure you don't want to stay? I'll order pizza," Libby asked as she let go of him.

He shook his head. "Naw, better eat something a little better. Vicki's been getting on me about my cholesterol and I'm sure the sausage and bacon this morning did me in."

"Are you sure?" Libby asked.

Dad smiled and patted her on the shoulder. "I'm sure."

"Well, thank you, Art. You really helped us a lot today."

He was talking to Libby, but looked directly at me. "Parents would do anything that's best for their kids."

Chapter 9

Going back to work after a long weekend sucked. But it sucked even more that it was the first day of my new job in New Orleans.

I left even earlier than usual. Libby was still sound asleep, curled up on her side with a set of pillows between her legs.

I would have given anything to be that pillow instead, but if she wanted things like new furniture, I had to take this job. I had to prove that I was the man who could provide for her.

It was still dark out as I drove my truck down the highway. None of the shops were open when I pulled into a small strip mall for one of those chain coffee places.

I would have just brought my normal Thermos of coffee and lunch, but I was too damn tired to even think about it and Libby still hadn't gone grocery shopping to restock our fridge. I needed to text her later to remind her to do that.

I stepped inside and stared at the menu board in front of me. Five dollars for some fancy coffee? Man, how did girls buy this shit all the time?

I ordered a large black coffee and some kind of breakfast sandwich thing and inwardly cringed when I pulled the large bill out of my wallet.

But nothing could make me cringe more than the person I saw when I stepped around the counter to wait for my order.

"Hey, I've never seen you here before,;slumming it in New Orleans?"

Julie's voice was perky. Too perky for this early in the morning.

She was wearing a purple button down shirt with a knee-length skirt and her hair pulled back into a tight bun. She looked like a professional. Or maybe one of those professional looking women in porn videos.

"I have a job on the new toll going in," I muttered, before yawning. Damn, I was going to have to start going to bed earlier.

"Oh, that's really cool. I didn't know you were working out this far. We should do lunch sometime."

I shook my head. "Naw, I usually have lunch real quick on site, then get back to work."

The guy behind the counter called both our names and set down my coffee and sandwich and some frou frou blended drink with a lot of whipped cream for Julie.

"Okay, how about having your cup with me now then? I have a few minutes to spare."

I looked at the guy behind the counter who wiggled his eyebrows then I rubbed the back of my neck as I turned to Julie and walked toward the door. "I don't know. I don't want to be late for my first day."

"Well, what time you do start?" She blinked those big green eyes at me.

"Seven."

Shit. I should have lied and said earlier, but my reflexes weren't on point that early in the morning.

She smiled and put her hand on my elbow. "Then we still have time for a quick cup. Please, Blaine? I just want to talk."

Her touch didn't give me the same tingles that it used to. That girl used to have a direct line to my libido, but then again I was a horny ass teenager when we dated. But even though there wasn't a spark, that didn't stop me from answering the thing I shouldn't have said.

I sighed. "Okay, one quick cup."

The smile broadened on her face and I followed her to a set of polka dot chairs in the corner. She took a long sip of her drink and crossed one leg over the other. "So, how long are you going to be working in New Orleans?"

I shrugged. "Whenever the job is done or they reassign me. It could be a few years. A few months. More than likely a few years."

She nodded. "Wow, that's going to be a long time to be away from Elsbury."

"Yeah, not too bad. This early it only takes me about forty minutes, if that."

She took another long sip of her drink. "What does Libby think about that?"

"She's fine with it."

"Libby really does seem like a nice girl, even though she hates me."

I laughed. "Can you blame her? You're kind of my cheating ex."

She winced. "I guess I deserve that, but to be fair, you may have not cheated with another girl, but I would say I was second in your life to your boys and baseball."

I couldn't help but laugh at the stupidity of comparing her sleeping with someone else to me and baseball. "Wow, that's a good one, Jules."

She shook her head and looked down at her hands. "I'm serious, Blaine. Half of our relationship was me sitting on the bench while you practiced, then sitting again at Sam's while you and your friends talked about stupid shit. If I was lucky you might fool around with me in the cab of your truck until my curfew. But that was it. We never talked. When we did it was mainly you talking about baseball."

"Oh, come on, I wasn't that bad and even if I was, I was young and stupid. What else was there to talk about besides baseball and our friends?"

She shrugged. "I don't know. You never really asked what I wanted. Do you even know why I chose to go to Ole Miss? Or that I actually hated being a cheerleader, but I was afraid I'd ruin my reputation if I quit the squad, even though the girls were bitches? No girl wanted to hang out with me because I spent so much time with you that there wasn't room for anyone else."

I blinked and went to shake my head, but the more I thought about it, the more that did make sense.

"Blaine, are you even listening to me?"

LSU was up by one and Ole Miss' best batter was up to bat. I didn't want to miss the play so my eyes were glued to the TV, even though Julie was shoving my arm, trying to get my attention.

"Yeah, hey, let me just watch this play."

The batter swung and the crack of the bat rang out before the ball went wide and into foul territory.

"Hell yeah. If that's the only thing he hits, I'll be happy."

The screen went black and I gasped without even thinking about what I was doing and turned to Julie, who sat with her arms crossed over her chest and her eyes narrowed. "Blaine, I'm trying to talk to you! Seriously, this is my last night here and all you want to do is watch a dumb game."

I shook my head and let out a single laugh. "It's not a dumb game. It's a very important game for LSU and they happen to be going against your college. Better brush up on your Crimson Tide, ma'am."

I poked her in the ribs and tickled right under her breastbone for good measure, but she didn't laugh. She didn't even crack a smile.

"Blaine. Seriously. I'm not going to see you for weeks and you've barely even looked at me all night."

"That's not true. We just went out to dinner and I've been with you since the moment I got off work."

She rolled her eyes. "Yeah, dinner at the drive-thru where you tried to feel me up the entire time, then the waitress flirted with you. And before that, it was a lot more groping and you getting interrupted every two seconds by texts from your friends asking if you were coming by."

"I know what this is..."

I scooted closer and put my arm around her. "You think I'm going to replace you with another woman while you're gone. I can promise you that you're my only girl, Jules."

She shoved my hand off. "Are you seriously even listening? That's not what I said at all!"

I groaned. "What do you want me to say? Can we just not fight? It's our last night together before you leave. I promise, this game only has a few more innings then we can watch whatever you want."

She sighed but nodded. I would have tried to figure out what was bugging her, hell, maybe even just gone down on her to see if that made her smile, but I really didn't want to miss the game.

"You're the best." I leaned in and kissed her cheek, then took the remote and turned the game back on.

I WAS THE YOUNGEST guy on site. It was one of the longest and most grueling days of working in the Louisiana heat.

Which made my day all that much worse.

All I could think about was what Julie said.

Was I really that bad of a boyfriend?

Hell, was I an even worse husband?

I didn't even notice the radio wasn't on when I drove to the high school in Elsbury. I parked and went to turn down the dial and stared at the blank screen.

Slowly, I rested my head against the steering wheel. Was I doing the right thing? Was it even worth it?

I rolled up my shirt sleeves. I didn't have time to run home and shower, so I'd changed into a button-down shirt and my khakis in the back of my car. I'd also put on a second coat of deodorant and the expensive cologne that Libby's sister got me for Christmas. Damn, now I really was smelling like a teenage boy. I didn't know if that was a good or a bad thing for getting the job.

"Okay, Crabtree, you can do this. You want this. You finally get to get back on the field."

I shook my head. Shit, now I was talking to myself? Maybe I'd had too much sun.

While work in Elsbury was breezy, in New Orleans I was the youngest guy by at least ten years and as the new guy, I had to do the grunt work. My hands were hurting and my muscles ached, but I wasn't going to pansy out.

Slowly, I got out of the car and stretched. School was still out for the summer, but the parking lot was packed with football players in for two-a-days. I sure as hell didn't miss that. At least with baseball we didn't start until the winter and that was just for indoor batting practice.

But I did play football. And that did take up my life for six months, then baseball did.

Maybe Julie was right.

I shook my head, even though I didn't say the feelings out loud. I couldn't think like that. I had to keep my head out of the clouds. This was game time and Coach would know if I didn't bring my best plays.

I crossed the paved parking lot and opened the doors closest to the gym. Coach's office was right outside of the boy's locker room, and I cringed from the familiar scent of too much men's body spray and sweat. I'd spent way too much time against the gray metal lockers, staring at the chipped green walls.

I'd also spent a lot of time in Coach's office. I knew the place well.

Three of his walls were covered in glass and faced the rest of the locker room. It was a small room that was crammed with a large metal desk and some folding chairs. Framed newspaper clippings and trophies covering the little bit of wall space.

Coach was hunched over his desk, his familiar LSU ball cap on his head as he stared down at some papers in front of him.

I knocked for formality, but I knew I could just walk in. I'd always done it.

Coach looked up and smiled, waving me in. "Crabtree, glad you made it!"

He stood up and we briskly shook hands. "Take a seat." He pointed toward one of the folding chairs across from him.

"Thank you, sir," I said and sat down.

Coach laughed. "Don't give me that 'sir', shit, Crabtree. I rode your ass for four years and now you're a grown ass man coming in for a job interview. You can still call me Coach or hell, you can call me Rene."

I smiled. There was no way in hell I could ever get used to calling the man by his first name. "Okay, Coach."

He sifted through the papers on his desk, then folded his hands on top of him. "Now you know this is just a formality to have you come in for the assistant job. I saw you out on the field with Brady Preston and I've seen you on the field as a pitcher. We both know you have the talent for it and no one else could compare."

I blinked hard. I wasn't expecting him to say any of that. Sure, I knew I was a great pitcher, but never expected Coach to actually admit it or to think I could be an assistant coach.

"The assistant position doesn't pay well. Actually, it barely pays anything. I was able to talk to the school board about giving a small stipend since you have a baby on the way."

I nodded. "Thank you si— I mean Coach."

I hadn't even accepted the job and he was acting like I had it. That I wanted it. The more I thought about it and my feet digging back in the sand, the more I did want it. Even though I should have probably discussed it with Libby. I guess I didn't expect an offer and knew we'd be in for one hell of a long talk when I got home.

"Now, to take over the head coach position, you would need some sort of teaching experience. You've got a little bit of time before I retire, and I know that Coach Murphy is looking to possibly hire on an assistant coach for JV football as well. If you started taking classes now, you could easily get your teaching degree within in four years, and then have enough experience to take over for us."

Holy hell. I blinked once then twice, my mouth going completely dry as I tried to form words. I'd never thought about being a coach, much less a teacher. I figured I'd be on the road crew forever and this would just be a hobby.

"That's awfully nice of you Coach, but I'm not sure I'm the teaching type." I rubbed the back of my neck.

He laughed. "Hell, son, when I was your age I didn't think I was good for anything else but hitting a ball. My coach sat down with me and did the same thing I'm doing for you. He found me scholarships and soon I was going to school part-time while working at the couplings factory. It sucked. It sucked hard, son. But after a year into it, and especially once I started student teaching, I knew this was where I belonged."

He leaned back. "Now I know you think that you're going to make shit as a teacher, but with stipends for coaching, you and the Mrs. could have a pretty good paycheck coming to you. You'd also have most of the summer off, except for practices in August, and be on the same schedule as your kids."

I sucked in a deep breath and let it out slowly. "Yeah. That would be nice."

He stood up and patted my shoulder. "I know it's a lot for you to think about, Crabtree, and you don't have to give me your answer right now, but the board wants it soon. Go home and talk to your wife. Talk to your friends. Hell, talk to your former teammates. Then get back to me by the end of this week, because I'm going to have to interview someone else and I'd hate to do that."

I swallowed hard, letting everything sink in. Coaching. Going to college. Teaching. All things I never associated with me. Now they were right in front of me and I had to make a decision if it was what I wanted to do.

"Thanks, Coach. I'll get back to you ASAP." I stood up and shook his hand.

He smiled and patted my back. "I know you will, son. I know you will."

MY HEAD WAS SWIMMING with information. So much that I just sat in my car for a few minutes, scrolling through my phone before I even left the parking lot.

I could take classes the same time as Libby at night and we could use a babysitter during the day. Or even work opposite schedules.

But when would I see her?

When would I see our son?

I sat the phone down and drove down Conger Road back to our house, still trying to wrap my head around everything.

Someone finally believed I was more than a set of muscles. That I could actually do something for other people. Hell, that meant more to me than anything else in my last twenty years.

If I was still living with my parents, I would probably jump on the opportunity, but now I had to think about the two other people in my life. Two other lives I had to support instead of just thinking about myself, which I had been doing all of my life.

When I pulled up to the front of the house, Jackson's truck was parked out front.

Shit. Was I supposed to do something with him and forgot and now Libby was in there, probably giving him the third degree?

I parked next to him and got out, running to the front door. I didn't expect to hear the sounds of a hammer and laughter.

I walked down the small hallway to the living room, where Libby and Jackson were both on all fours, locking in wooding flooring. They hooked in another board before Libby looked up and smiled, jumping up and running over to greet me.

"Hey, Blaine! How was the first day? And the interview?" She looped her arms around me in a big hug, almost making me feel guilty for being gone so long. And for having coffee with Julie that morning. But I wasn't going to ever tell Libby that last part.

"It was long. Really long."

Jackson stood up, wiping off his hands. "Yeah, that's the last time I'm letting you be gone late. Your wifey here couldn't wait any longer to get in this floor so she called Dina to help, who of course was working and called me."

I looked down at the dark wooden floor that took up half the living room. There was still a lot of work to be done but they had a good start. "Thanks, brother, I appreciate you helping out."

He laughed, patting my back. "Libby didn't give me much of a choice."

I put my arm around Libby. "Yeah, she's pretty convincing."

Libby squealed when I pinched her side.

Jackson shook his head. "And on that note, I'm going to take off before you two christen these floors and try to get Libby pregnant again."

"Oh, come on, Jacks. I owe you dinner or something for helping out," I yelled.

Jackson just smiled. "Naw, I'm sure you'll return the favor when I need help."

With that he put on his boots and headed out the front door.

As soon as he was gone, Libby spun around to face me. "Sooo...how did the interview go? Are you the new coach?"

I rubbed the back of my head. "Well, not exactly. Coach said I basically had the job, but he wants me to look into going back to school, since an assistant usually needs teaching experience. He said that I could have a few years, and then when that was up, I could start teaching there and take over his job."

Libby's eyes widened. "Wow, you want to teach and you never told me?"

I shrugged. "I didn't know that I did. I still don't."

"Well, that's kind of what college is for. You go and figure out what you like and don't like. If you don't like your teaching classes or this coaching job then you do something else."

I sighed. "Baby, I barely got through high school. I only did because Coach helped me out."

She smiled. "Well, then you could be that same coach to do that for another kid. I think it's a great opportunity."

"But I still need to work. We both do. How the hell am I supposed to support us if I don't?"

She chewed on her bottom lip. "Well, we could work around each other's schedules. I just signed up for my spring semester. I only have four classes left and I was able to get them all at night. 6-8:50 Monday through Thursday. You can still work most of the day and do one or two classes at night or after work, head on over to a class."

"Monday through Thursday all night? If I stay working in New Orleans, when am I supposed to see you?"

She looked at the clock above our stove. "Well, hopefully you would be home at seven every night and if not, then I'll be here after nine."

"Who is watching Mathieu?"

"I've got that all figured out. Your mom has off on Mondays, so she can watch him when we work during the day. Aunt Dee said I could do the accounting from home on Tuesdays and Wednesdays. Thursdays Dina has off and said she could help out and Britt said she could help watch him anytime you're working late and I need to leave."

My head was spinning. All these plans revolved around me working late and handing off our kid to someone else. Maybe Coach was right about getting on the same schedule as our kid. And if I was leaving every morning by five and getting home at seven, there was no way in hell I was going to see Libby by the time she got home from school. I'd be passed the hell out.

Something was going to need to change.

But I tried to keep those thoughts off my face.

"That all sounds great, baby." I leaned in and kissed her forehead. "Now, let's get something to eat, then you can watch me finish these floors."

Chapter 10

I was completely running on empty.

Two nights with only three hours of sleep, so I could finish the floors, then working twelve hour days in the sun was wearing on me.

And now I only had two more days to figure out if I was going to take the coaching job.

Instead of spending the night discussing it with Libby, we were going over to her Aunt Dee's for supper.

"So what's the occasion for dinner tonight?" I stared over at Libby who was holding her tray of deviled eggs like it was the Holy Grail and she was afraid to drop it at any moment. Aside from bacon, she was now always craving eggs and I'd had more recipes with eggs in them the last few weeks than I ever wanted in my life.

"She just said it would be nice to have us over since we've all been so busy."

I nodded. Dee was always a sweet lady. She'd had it rough most of her life with an addict daughter who abandoned her granddaughter. I always wondered why she agreed to take Libby in in the first place, but it was never my place to ask.

We pulled up to Dee's small, shotgun style house that was only about a mile from our place. I guess that would be good if Britt and Dee were going to be watching Mathieu at all. None of my family was too far and with them down the road, it would definitely help. Now if only Libby and I would actually find time to see each other and our kid, that would be the best situation.

Dee stepped out onto the front porch and waved us in.

She'd always been pretty spry for an older lady, but once we got inside, I noticed she wasn't moving as fast and her usually colored red hair was now streaking with gray.

Shit.

This was going to be one of those dinners in which she told us she was sick and that Britt was going to move in with us when hospice came in.

I knew it.

"Dee, you look lovely as always," I said, giving her a big hug, but making sure not to squeeze her too tight.

"Oh, well thank you Blaine. Sorry, I've been a little under the weather."

I waved my hand. "Well, you look great and I'm sure it's nothing that a little chicken noodle soup and some good Gris Gris can't fix."

Dee smiled and put her hand on my shoulder before she turned and went back to the kitchen.

Her house was small, but really not that much smaller than mine and Libby's. It just looked smaller because the outdated yellow kitchen ran smack dab into the family room that was full of way too much furniture. Just looking over the two rooms, my head was spinning with ways I could improve it. First thing would be to knock down a few walls.

"Hey, y'all." Libby's cousin Britt walked out of the back room.

I'd known Britt since she was just a little thing, hanging on Dee's leg at every school function. She grew into a tomboy that was the best softball catcher in the parish. If she wanted to, she could easily get a scholarship.

"Britt, what's going on with your hair?" Libby ruffled her fingers through Britt's short, spiky black hair that now had streaks of blue in it.

Britt put her hand to her head. "Just a little something some of the other girls on the team were doing. Grandma already lectured me on it."

"Don't worry, I'm not going to scold you too. I'm just saying, it's not my style," Libby said.

Britt laughed. "What are you going to do when little Matty comes home with blue hair?"

Libby shook her head. "First off, he will not be called Matty and second off, his daddy will probably have his hide if he did that."

Britt held onto her stomach and laughed. "I doubt Blaine would do that. He's still keeping up with that blond do, so he has no room to talk."

I ran my fingers through my hair. It was badly needing a cut and probably to touch up my roots. My mom first started dying it blond when I was in middle school. The girls thought I looked like a boy bander and started giving me their numbers left and right, so I kept it. But I guess at twenty, it was starting to look a little stupid.

Libby took my hand and kissed my knuckles. "Blond is different than blue. And it looks cute on Blaine."

Britt made a gagging noise.

"Now, stop fighting y'all and let's eat before the fish gets cold. No one wants to eat cold catfish," Dee yelled, before setting the big tray on the table.

"Here, let me help you, ma'am." I grabbed the other bowls of black eyed peas and grits and set them on the table.

"You're always so helpful, Blaine. My Libby is lucky to have you." Dee smiled, patting my back as we sat down.

"You should see the way he's been working Aunt Dee. He took down all the cabinets in the kitchen and made them into a new dresser and side tables for our bedroom. I'm sure the man can do anything with his hands," Libby said, smiling and rubbing my back like a proud mother hen.

Britt laughed, almost choking on her sweet tea. "Yeah, I'm sure he's good with his hands."

Dee swatted Britt's leg, but it had the same effect as fly swatting an elephant. "Brittany! Manners!"

"Sorry, Grandma," Britt muttered, putting her head down.

"Okay, now let's pray so we can dig in," Dee said, grabbing Britt and Libby's hands. Libby held onto my other hand and I took Britt's free hand as we bowed our heads.

Dee recited the Catholic prayer and we all kind of followed along before we said 'Amen' in unison and then let go of each other's hand and started digging in.

"So, how's work on the road crew going, Blaine? Libby tells me you're working in New Orleans now," Dee said as she scooped some grits onto her plate.

"It's going all right. Hot and a lot of work, but it's going," I said, watching Dee for any signs of tremors or something that would show weakness.

"He's actually been asked to be the new assistant baseball coach for Elsbury," Libby said, staring at Dee with a broad smile on her face.

It was a good subject change, but that still left the spotlight on me.

Dee clasped her hands together. "Oh, that's wonderful, Blaine! Maybe you'll even get to help Britt and the girls' team."

"Let's not get ahead of ourselves. I haven't accepted the job yet." I folded and unfolded my napkin for something to do with my hands.

"But you're going to, right?" Libby asked, staring at me with those big puppy dog eyes.

I blew out a big breath of air and rubbed the back of my neck. "I don't know. Maybe."

"Well, what's holding you back?" Dee asked, adjusting her Coke bottle glasses.

"Coach said I'd have to get my degree and start teaching in the next few years. I guess he was able to get me a stipend and approval for me to start out without schooling, but I'd have to be employed by the school if I ever wanted the head coaching position."

"Well, that sounds like a mighty fine idea, Blaine. Then you wouldn't have those long hours in the heat anymore on the road crew. Why, you could even be a shop teacher if you like working on all of those projects," Dee offered with a tight-lipped smile.

I took a sip of my sweet tea. I hadn't even thought about doing something like that. Coach was our gym teacher and I figured that was what I'd be stuck doing. That or maybe history or some other classroom environment. None of those options sounded appealing. But teaching something where I got to still work with my hands, now that actually sounded promising.

"I don't know, Dee. I guess we'll see what happens when Mathieu is born and Libby's out of school." I put my hand on Libby's knee.

Dee set her fork down and smoothed out her dress. "I guess that leads me into why I wanted y'all here tonight."

I raised an eyebrow. I knew it. I knew there was going to be an ulterior motive. I glanced over at Libby, who was biting her bottom lip.

"What is it, Aunt Dee? Is everything okay?"

She smiled and patted Libby's hand. "Everything's fine, dear. Well, sort of."

Dee sighed, which made her look even older with the wrinkles creasing around her eyes. "I'm getting older. I thought I could run the shop forever, but truth be told, I know that my arthritis is getting too bad to do inventory all day. With you taking over the books, it's helped, but still not enough."

"Aunt Dee, if you need me to come into the shop more and help you, I can. I promise," Libby said, putting her hand on Dee's.

I held my breath. How the hell was that going to happen? We were already struggling as it was trying to get everything juggled between my work and her school, with a baby on the way, we definitely wouldn't see each other if she was working more.

Dee smiled. "I had something else in mind. I've been talking to my estate attorney and he agrees with me, that we should set up a trust and have you slowly buy the shop from me."

Libby's eyebrows shot up. "What? You want me to take over the shop? Aunt Dee, I don't know anything about running a business!"

And neither did I. Hell, half the time I didn't even feel like I was enough of a grown up to live in my own house. But, I guess marriage and becoming a parent has a way of thrusting you into those types of things.

Dee put her hands down. "Now, I'm not saying you have to do it right away. We can build up to it. You can still finish school and I'll start teaching you the ropes. I know that you'll have your own ideas and you can probably turn the shop into the quaint little place I'd always wanted it to be instead of the pawn shop it's become. I just ask that you keep Dina on and Marion, until she decides to retire as well."

Libby winced. She'd complained about Marion more than once and the fact that she always said she was doing inventory, but would be watching cat videos on her phone or the computer.

Dee gently swatted Libby's leg. "Now, don't sass. Marion has been with me since the beginning and Dina knows a thing or two about business."

Libby let out a big breath. "Wow. This is a lot, Aunt Dee. I don't know what to think."

Dee patted Libby's hand. "You don't have to decide right now, but I'd like you to seriously consider it. There's no one else I'd rather have taking over the shop than you."

I opened my mouth to say something, but shut it when I felt my phone vibrating in my pocket. I was afraid it was going to be Coach asking about my decision, when I had no idea how in the hell this was going to change things with Libby taking over the shop. But it wasn't Coach's name flashing across the screen.

Julie: Hey, seeing if you'd be up for coffee tomorrow again. I have an errand to run for my boss before work.

Julie?

I didn't even know she still had my number.

I should have ignored it. I should have been paying attention to my wife, but instead I found myself texting back.

Sure, sounds great.

"Who are you texting?" Libby asked.

I stuffed my phone back in my pocket. "Just Jackson seeing if I could meet up with him at Reesey's."

I hated lying to Libby, but I figured that was better than telling her the truth.

"Oh, don't tell him about the shop! I don't want him telling Dina." Libby blinked.

God, I felt even worse about lying when she looked at me like that, her eyes focused and a small tinge of a smile on her lips, even though there was still worry lining them.

"I won't, baby. Don't worry."

"You're the best." She squeezed my leg and I felt even worse about not telling her who really texted me.

"Hey, who are you texting?" Nikki leaned over my shoulder and I shoved my phone back in my pocket.

I'd taken Dee's niece and her cousin home from Jackson's parents and stopped over at Nikki's. She had been blowing up my phone all night. I guess it didn't help that I was supposed to meet up with her the party and I left with Libby.

Now Libby was texting me.

Thanks again for the ride.

I put my number in her phone, thinking more with my dick at the time that she'd be up for some summer fun. Now just seeing her name and those five little words made a whole different sensation flow through me. One I hadn't felt for awhile.

"It's no one," I lied.

"Whoever it is, you seem to be awfully interested. Is it that RaeLynn bitch again? I don't know why you ever thought it was a good idea to get mixed up with her. Butch said she was crazy, even though I think he's getting back with her again."

I shook my head. "No. It's not RaeLynn. Don't worry about it."

"Okay, then maybe I should be worried about something else..." She shoved her hand down my pants and instead of getting excited, I pushed her off without even thinking about it.

"What the hell, Blaine?"

"I'm just not in the mood."

She rolled her eyes. "Since when are you not in the mood?"

"Since now," I growled and stood up. We were sitting on her back dock, where we normally fooled around.

Usually I would have been all up for it. I would have let her give me a hand job or whatever she wanted then went home to sleep it off, but tonight I didn't want any of it.

"What, now you're too good for me?"

"No. It's not that." I sighed. "Look, I've gotta work early in the morning, I'll catch you later, okay?"

She nodded, but there was a sadness in her eyes. The same sadness as the day I told her that I didn't want a girlfriend and then she still went down on me in the back of her truck. She might have said we were just friends, but I knew this girl wanted something more.

But if I was willing to hide texts from another girl and found my heart beating faster whenever I thought about Libby, then it was time to give up Nikki.

At least for the moment.

"I THINK THAT I SHOULD see if Dina wants to go in as partners with me at the shop."

I was knocked out of my thoughts by Libby's words. I slowed down the car and glanced in her direction. "What?"

"I think that it would be a good idea if I did this with Dina. She knows the business and I think she could really help with me finishing school and getting everything settled with Mathieu."

I shook my head. "I don't know, baby, are you sure you want to get into a business deal with a friend?"

She let out a puff of air. "No, but I think that Dina should have probably gotten the business over me. I know Aunt Dee is only giving it to me because I'm family, but it's Dina's baby. I think she could at least help me for a while and if we want to expand and do a second shop in Caimon or something, we could do that. I think whenever I talk to Aunt Dee and her lawyer, I'm going to suggest it."

I put my hand on her thigh and squeezed gently. "If that's what you think is best."

"This will also help when you go back to school. I could have some wiggle room at the shop with someone else to help me run it. Then I could take some more time at home with Mathieu while you're at school and vice versa."

I licked my lips. "Baby, I'm not even sure if I want to take Coach's offer."

"Why not? You love baseball. You always have and I saw you talking to that pitcher, you're a damn good coach. I also know you'll be a great teacher. Hell, Britt and her friends adore you and every guy in this town looks up to you. If you go to school, take a few classes and hate it, then you can try something else. But you won't know any of that unless you try."

I looked full-on at my girl. All this time I'd been thinking about how this was going to affect me and possibly our family and that I'd probably fail. But she'd failed so many times and then picked herself back up again to succeed. If anyone was going to be my constant cheerleader, it was her.

Which made me feel even worse about meeting up with Julie. I was going to have to delete her number from my phone.

"Okay, baby. I'll call Coach tomorrow and look into when I can sign up for classes at St. Joseph."

She squealed and reached over and hugged me, causing me to swerve a bit. "Oops, sorry!"

Libby went back to her seat.

I laughed and put my arm around her, pulling her closer. "Nothing to be sorry about. I like seeing you excited."

She kissed my jaw line. "And I like seeing you happy."

Chapter 11

The first week of work in New Orleans had finally finished. All I wanted to do was stay home and relax.

But that wasn't going to happen.

Mom and my sisters were throwing a baby shower at my parents' and decided to make it a couples' shower, which meant my presence was mandatory.

At least the girls made it a barbecue. I was deathly afraid I was going to walk into a room full of blue ribbon and baby bottle decorations, but I guess Mom knew me better than I thought.

The backyard was set up with a few picnic tables and when we got there. Dad was hanging a set of twinkling lights and blue streamers from the willows.

"Blaine, Libby, you're here and early!" Mom said, as she set out a tray of hamburger meat on the table next to the grill.

"Of course we are. This all looks wonderful, Vicki," Libby said, giving her a big hug.

Libby seemed to get bigger every day and in her flowy blue dress, she looked like she would pop at any moment. But I didn't tell her that. I just kissed her forehead and always told her that she looked beautiful.

And I was probably the biggest piece of shit.

Julie had still been texting me and I'd be lying if said that I wasn't texting her back.

I don't know why I was even doing it.

They seemed innocent enough.

Julie: You'd think New Orleans would be fun at night, but it's actually boring unless you're a drunk tourist.

Me: I bet.

Well, most of them.

Julie: Sometimes I hate lying in bed alone. It would be nice to have someone with me.

It never got any more heated than that, but I knew that it could. The problem was, I didn't know how to stop it.

Okay, so I could have just stopped texting her back and I vowed that I would.

Eventually.

There was just something. I don't know. Maybe I was waiting to get some closure for what happened between us or something like that. I really couldn't figure it out.

But Julie wasn't the only ghosts of girlfriends past that liked to show up.

Just when I thought things were going well with my family and friends coming to the party, in walked Butch Sinclair holding a thirty pack and on his arm was RaeLynn, his on-again-off-again girlfriend that I also happened to screw around with on more than one occasion. The last time I saw her with Libby at the barbecue joint she worked at, it wasn't so pretty.

"Fancy seeing you here Blaine Crabtree." My eyes almost bugged out of my head when I saw RaeLynn standing there in a stained barbecue t-shirt and short shorts. Her hair was pulled back away from her face and that only accentuated her permanent scowl. The girl had resting bitch face like no other.

"Heyya, RaeLynn," I tried to say it as casually as I could, but hell, I was sweating bullets. Last time I saw her, she was leaving the back of my truck with her panties balled in her hands. It was a mistake to screw her when she was on a break with Butch, but I was a little tipsy, she was a little slutty, and well...

"Haven't seen you around these parts in a while." Her eyes locked on me like she was trying to pry something out of my mouth. Shit. Why did I

pick this place? I should have taken Libby to a barbecue joint in Caimon or something.

I scratched the back of my neck and could feel myself actually sweating as it dripped into my eyebrows. "Yeah, I didn't know you were still working here."

"Of course I'm still working here. Where the hell else did you think I'd gone? There ain't much else in this town."

"Well, it's good to see that you are still working," I said, because I really didn't know what else I could say and I wasn't about to cause a scene.

Her nose flared up as she sucked in a deep breath of air. "I guess if you're gonna stick around here, you probably want something to eat. Sweet tea for you, as usual?"

I nodded. "Yeah, that's fine."

I looked over to Libby, hoping maybe the death glare would stop, or at least I could maybe stop focusing on it if I looked at her instead of RaeLynn. Too bad Libby was looking at me like I just told her I killed someone. "Baby, do you want sweet tea as well?"

"Yeah, that's fine," Libby squeaked. Shit. I hoped that RaeLynn wouldn't cause a scene and try to start a girl fight in the middle of the restaurant. She was captain of the girls' wrestling team in high school and I knew she could throw down.

"And who might you be, Blondie?" RaeLynn stared at Libby like she was the lowliest bug on the bottom of her shoe. That definitely lit something inside of me. No one looked at my girl like that. She wasn't just some fling. She was mine.

"Um, I'm Libby Gentry."

"My girlfriend," I added, hoping it wouldn't cause RaeLynn to attack her, but at least know where she stood.

RaeLynn's eyes widened to twice their normal size, then she looked from Libby to me before her eyes rested on me. "I thought you said you didn't do girlfriends?" she practically spat.

I shrugged, trying to be as nonchalant as possible, though at that point I was pretty sure she was looking to rip my eyeballs out. "Sometimes things change."

RaeLynn opened her mouth to say something else, but before she could someone yelled from behind me, "RaeLynn, you gonna come get these orders, or do I have to find someone else?"

"I'm coming!" RaeLynn yelled, turned on her heels, and disappeared through the door.

Libby let out a deep breath. "Well, that was interesting."

"Yeah, I'm sorry about that." I raked my hands through my hair, searching for something to say. "I forgot she worked here. We can go somewhere else if you'd like."

Libby shook her head. "No, it seems like this just is going to happen more and more."

I raised my eyebrows. I didn't want anything to come between me and Libby and I was kicking myself. Why the hell didn't I find this girl that made me weak years ago? Instead, I was busy screwing around with girls who did nothing but bring me down. I reached across the table and put my hand on hers. "Libby, come on. My sweet petite. You know none of these old girls mean anything to me. I wouldn't have introduced you as my girlfriend if I cared what they thought about us. You know I'm yours. No one else's."

She tucked a curl behind her ear. There was something about the sweet movement that made me smile even if it was brief. "Some days I think that, and some days I wonder how many of your exes I'm going to have to face."

"Hey, it wasn't much of a picnic for me to meet that guy at Kristi's wedding either," I grumbled.

She rolled her eyes. "Yeah, one ex. That's all I've got. You seem to have slept with half the town."

I pulled my hand back and frowned. "Hey, baby, that ain't fair. I thought we agreed that was in the past is the past, and the future is now."

"It doesn't help when your past keeps showing up in a pair of short shorts."

I growled, clenching my fists. I didn't want to argue. Not here. Not ever. I should have known this was a bad idea. "Libby, I don't know how many times I've got to tell you that these girls meant nothing to me back then, and they mean nothing to me now. They were all just flings. You're my sweet petite. No one else."

"So that's all I was? A stupid fling?"

I whipped my head to see RaeLynn standing next to our table with two foam cups in her hands.

I turned toward her, holding my hands up, palms out. Maybe reasoning would work. "Hey, you knew we was just having some fun when we got together. You were just getting over Butch Sinclair, and I was just getting over Julie."

"You take me muddin', fuck me, and then never call me again! If that's what you call a fling then fuck you Blaine Crabtree, because you were nothing but a ride in the truck for me, too!" With that, she took both of the foam cups and dumped them over my head. I gasped as the cool, brown liquid streamed over my face and down my shirt, soaking into my skin. I wiped my face as RaeLynn turned on her boots and stormed out.

"I think it's time to go," Libby whispered.

I nodded, sweet tea dripping from every part of me. "I think that's probably a good idea."

And if it wasn't enough to have RaeLynn with Butch, running in behind them was Nikki wearing a pretty skimpy pink dress and carrying a big box of diapers.

Shit. Shit. Shit.

I left Libby's side and ran over to them, hoping maybe I could at least run some interference. "Hey, y'all, didn't know you were coming." I raked my hands through my hair and tried to will myself not to start sweating through my dress shirt. It was middle of July and I was going to sweat anyway, but this was making it about a million times worse.

Butch handed me the thirty-pack. "Yeah, I didn't know baby showers were for dudes, but when Meg brought her car in the other day she told me it was for couples. I asked what to get y'all and she said beer and diapers, so we came prepared."

"I'm sure these will both come in handy." I forced the biggest, toothiest grin I could.

RaeLynn's face didn't break into anything more than her permanent scowl as she tossed her long black hair over her shoulder. "Congratulations. I didn't even know y'all were hitched."

"Yeah. June 11th. I guess you could say that we move quickly." I laughed nervously because I didn't know what the hell else to do.

Butch squeezed RaeLynn's shoulder. "Yeah, baby, remember I told you about the wedding and you said it would be a cold day in hell before you ever went to Blaine Crabtree's wedding."

Butch laughed, tossing his head back. "Hell, Crabtree, you don't know how much time I had to spend south of her border just to get her to come today."

RaeLynn squeezed his side and the string bean of a man in flannel practically went to his knees. The girl had one hell of a grip. "Hush up, Butch."

"Ow, ow. Sorry, baby!"

She let go of him and he stood back up, shaking his shaggy black hair. "And of course Nikki wanted to come too, I think this is her peace offering."

RaeLynn smacked him in the stomach and he let out a big whoosh of air. "You need to learn to keep your mouth shut, Butch. You're just making things worse."

I shook my head. "Hey, we all knew this would be awkward, right? Thank y'all for coming. I appreciate it."

Nikki didn't even look in my direction. She just kept her head down, biting her bottom lip.

A tug came at my arm and I looked to see Libby with her fake smile plastered on her face. I hated that smile. It was the one she used when she was trying to be nice but really wanted to slap someone in the face. "Blaine, your mom wants us over at the table. Your dad is going to say grace before we eat and get the party started."

"Okay, baby, sounds good." I took her hand as she pulled me away.

"What the hell are they doing here?" she hiss-whispered as we walked toward the food table.

"I guess Meg invited Butch, and he and RaeLynn are back together."

"And Nikki?" Libby raised her eyebrows.

"I'm thinking she just came because Butch is here, or maybe she wants to apologize for making a drunken fool of herself at the wedding. I'm sure she didn't mean what she said."

Libby rolled her eyes. "Alcohol is like a truth serum. She totally meant what she said. She may not have meant to say it, but she did."

I put my arm around her shoulder. "Hey, I know what she said was mean, but let's try and move past it. She's here today, so let's just be civil and enjoy everyone who is here to celebrate the upcoming arrival of Mathieu."

Libby groaned. "I wish he was coming sooner. My feet are killing me. I'm so swollen that I'm getting cankles."

I didn't want to look down and see if it was true.

"Well, I'm sure I can give you a nice foot massage later."

She smiled as I leaned in to kiss her forehead. "You'd better."

We made our way over to the buffet table where Mom and Dad had a spread of burgers, hot dogs, different chips, potato salad, and of course a big ol' alligator cake that they had especially made for us from one of mom's clients.

Dad stood at the table with Mom on one side and Libby and I on the other. Everyone else stood around the picnic tables that were covered with blue plastic table cloths and bouquets of crepe myrtles in the center. Even without Libby's parents' money, Mom and Dad still made it look nice in their backyard. I knew that the tables were either our old ones from the shed or borrowed from people that my parents knew from church or work and that most of the decorations came from the discount party store in New Orleans. It wasn't the grand tent, rented tables, and over the top flowers that we had at our wedding, but it was still nice and I think Libby was happy with it as well.

Dad put his hands together and bowed his head. "Lord, thank you for bringing our friends and family here with us to celebrate the upcoming birth of the newest little Crabtree, Mathieu. We ask that you bless this food we are about to eat and that you continue to bless our family and friends as they continue on this journey with us. Amen."

Everyone responded with "Amen".

Dad looked up at me and smiled, then turned to everyone and raised his hands. "Let's eat!"

Libby and I piled our plates before taking a seat at a table with my parents, Aunt Dee, and Britt. My sisters, their husbands, and kids had to sit at a different table, but I could still hear my niece, Abby, screaming that she didn't want no stinking 'tato salad'.

Mom stood up and lifted up a clear glass with a blue liquid in it. Dad clinked the vase on the table to get everyone's attention. "Okay, y'all, I know some of you hate shower games, but this one's easy and we have some real nice prizes for the ladies and the men. Now y'all need to look at your glasses, where you'll see some ice cubes with little plastic babies in them. Once the ice cube breaks and the baby pops out, you need to yell 'my water broke!' The first person to have their water break wins a prize."

"Let's hope it's not Libby," Dad said and everyone laughed.

Libby held her stomach. "Nope. Mathieu is staying in there for as long as he needs to."

Mom sat back down on the picnic bench. "I'm surprised you're still saying that. With this heat, girl, I'd be wanting that baby out as soon as possible."

Libby shook her head. "I am just fine with him being all safe and sound in there because as soon as he's out, I think there's going to be chaos."

Aunt Dee squeezed her hand. "Oh, it won't be that bad. You'll have all of our help."

Libby took a sip of her drink. "You didn't see my sister after she had her baby."

But I did.

"Hi, Beth, how are you feeling?" Libby leaned over and kissed her sister's cheek.

Last time I saw Beth she looked like a walking Barbie with her shiny pink dress and her hair blown out like a Texas Beauty queen. But now she sat there looking more like Linda Blair in The Exorcist with dark circled eyes, messy hair, and a huge ass scowl.

"Honestly? I haven't slept, my boobs hurt, and my lady bits feel like they're on fire. I don't know why in the hell you thought this would be a good idea to do this, too," Beth snapped.

"I'm sure we're going to be just fine," I said, squeezing Libby's knee. Maybe I wasn't exactly sure if that was true, but it felt like the right thing to say.

After eating and serving the alligator cake, Mom and Dad made us sit on a set of folding chairs, surrounded by our gifts that I guess we were supposed to open in front of everyone. I thought that was weird and almost rude. I didn't want to make anyone feel bad if someone got us something better than the other person. I didn't even want to tell my mama that Libby's parents sent us our nursery furniture, but I was pretty sure Dad told her.

Libby picked up a blue bag with white polka dots on it. She opened up a tiny card that was attached with white ribbon. "Okay, this first one is from Jackson and Dina."

I looked over the crowd and waved at Jackson, who nodded to me with his arm around Dina. They stood in the back next to Butch and

RaeLynn. At their side was Nikki, who still had her head down. I didn't know why she bothered to come at all. She hadn't said a single word, which scared me even more. I hoped she just wasn't waiting for the right moment to get a little crazy. There wasn't any alcohol, but I was sure that Dad had a keg somewhere or some cans that he'd probably bring out as things winded down.

Hopefully if he did, Nikki would be gone by then.

Libby pulled out some tissue paper from the bag and pulled out a box. "Bottles for Mathieu..." She set them on the ground and then pulled a six pack of beer from the bottom of the bag. "And I guess these bottles are for Blaine?"

Everyone laughed, but I found my cheeks growing hot. I wasn't an alcoholic or anything and definitely wasn't expecting this much beer at a party. Especially not a baby shower where the parents-to-be were only twenty.

That also wasn't the first or last bottle I got. Every gift seemed to come with something cutesy for the baby and then something alcoholic for me. By the time we were done opening gifts, we had enough that we could open our own bar.

"Wait, there's one more thing!" Mom stood up and signaled to my dad.

Dad nodded then ran around to the side of the house, before slowly coming back out, pushing a big blue jogging stroller that was filled with baby clothes, toys, and stuffed animals. One in particular I recognized in the middle.

Dad stopped it in front of Libby and Mom walked over, picking up the raggedy brown teddy bear that was wrapped in a new quilted blue blanket with the words 'Crabtree' embroidered on it in green.

"This here, Libby, is Mister Bear. This was Blaine's first teddy bear. He slept in his crib every night when he was a baby and went to school with Blaine every day in his backpack until he was at least eight-years-old."

Mom wiped away a tear on her cheek and Libby's were falling freely from her eyes, so I put my arm around her, trying to keep my own feelings at bay.

"When Blaine first told me y'all were having a baby, I didn't know what to think, honestly. I just thought that I was going to lose my last baby. So I went up in Blaine's room while he was out buying you a ring. I made his bed for the last time and I found something in his sheets. Mister Bear was still there under his pillow after all of these years."

Some guys laughed in the crowd, but it didn't faze Mom. She petted Mister Bear's ears, looking down at him lovingly. "It reminded me that even though my baby's all grown up, there's still a part of him that always needs that comfort. That little thing that still makes him my baby. Now that he's having his own baby, I figured it was time that Mister Bear found a new home and that Mathieu would take good care of him."

Mom took the little swaddled bear and handed it to Libby who whispered, "I'll take good care of your baby and grandbaby, Vicki."

Mom leaned over and embraced Libby. "I know you will, sweetheart. I know you will."

She let go of Libby and looked at me with tears streaking her face. "You'll take good care of Mister Bear, okay? Let Mathieu know that he may not look as nice as some of the other bears, but he's real special."

I sniffled, trying to hold back tears. I wasn't going to pansy-out, but there was something about Mom's touching statement that had me trying not to crumble. "He already knows, Ma. He already knows."

THE SHOWER WAS DYING down. Since I wasn't about to break into the alcohol for the guests to enjoy, a lot of our friends left and the last ones around were Dina and Jackson.

At least I thought they were, until I was saying goodbye to Aunt Dee and Britt and felt a tap on my shoulder.

I whirled around to see Nikki standing there with her hands folded.

"Nikki? I thought you left with Butch and RaeLynn."

She shook her head. "No. I took my own truck. I was going to see if y'all needed any help."

I groaned. "Look, Nikki, I see what you're trying to do here, but Libby's pretty hormonal and I don't think now is the time for you to try and get in her good graces or whatever you're doing."

"I-I-I'm just here to help, really Blaine. I made an ass of myself at your wedding and I want to show that I support you two," Nikki said, stammering each word.

I shook my head. "That's all well and good that you want to do that and I appreciate it, but right now isn't the time. I think you should leave."

Nikki blinked. "You're not even going to give me a chance?"

I groaned. "Nikki, you basically told me that my wife and I weren't going to work. That wasn't the first time you've attacked her. I know we've been friends for a while, but I just don't' want any trouble, okay? I really am happy with Libby, despite what you and everyone else might think. She's not holding me back, in fact she's making me better."

And there was nothing truer. I thought for a while that maybe I was losing out on time with the guys, but the way she was pushing me to go for the coaching job and school, made me realize how much of a shitty husband I was being by complaining. She really was the best.

She put her hands on her hips. "So, really, just like that you're going to give up our years of friendship and tell me you don't want me around because of a mistake?"

"Sometimes mistakes happen and sometimes they're hard to get over. It's going to take some time, if it happens at all."

Now I wasn't sure if I was talking about Nikki or Julie. They'd both wronged me and yet I still couldn't seem to get either of them out of my life. Now was my chance to at least get one out.

"If you want me to leave, Blaine, just tell me."

I couldn't even look at her as I pointed toward the front of the house. "Leave, Nikki and don't come back."

Same for you, Julie. Don't come back.

I may have said that in my head, but I knew this was prepping me for the same talk I had to have with Julie. I was a married man and had to stand up for myself and my family. No crazy exes. No distractions. The past is the past. The future is now.

I didn't look up until she was half-way up to the house, running with her head down.

"Was that Nikki leaving?" Libby asked.

I put my arm around her. "Yeah. I don't think we're going to be seeing her for a while."

Libby raised an eyebrow. "And are you happy about that?"

I licked my lips and tilted my head. "What?"

She shrugged. "I mean, yeah I think she's a straight up, raging bitch and went all crazy drunk girl at our wedding, but I know you kind of like her family. I know she's your friend."

I shook my head. "Who are you and what have you done with my wife?"

She sighed. "I just want you to be happy, Blaine, to not hold you back."

I put my arms around her waist and turned her toward me. "Baby, you're not holding me back. You and Mathieu are the best thing that ever happened to me and I mean that. You make me a better me."

She smiled. "I'd lean in and kiss you for being so sweet, but I'm afraid there's a little bump in our way."

I turned her to the side and pressed my lips to her temple. "I know a few other positions we can try."

My sister Meg slapped the back of my head as she walked by. "Knock it off you two, we already know how the baby was conceived."

Libby and I shared a laugh, then I put my arm back around her. "I'm serious, okay? I am happy."

She nodded and smiled. "I'm happy too."

And I prayed she really was.

Chapter 12

"*No. Blaine. I'm pregnant. Pregnant with your child. It's why I've been so sick lately and it's not going to get better for probably another seven months and then I'll have someone else to take care of.*"

All the air felt like it had been sucked out of my lungs. My eyes lingered to her stomach. She had to be joking. It was still perfectly as flat as always. "You're shitting me."

She shook her head and put her shirt down. "No. I'm not shitting you. I'm pregnant. Knocked up."

I swallowed hard. One time. One time we had sex without a condom. It felt amazing. I'd wanted to do it again. Hell, I thought she had to have been on the pill. Every girl was. "How? Are you sure?"

She rolled her eyes. "Yes, I'm sure. The doctor tested me. She said she'll have the blood test back soon to give me a closer approximation, but I'm guessing around six weeks since that's when we had sex in the closet and you kind of didn't pull out."

I shook my head and couldn't take my eyes off her stomach. This couldn't be possible. This was the shit they made movies about, not that happened in real life. "I didn't know it could happen with just one time."

She glared at me, her nose turning up. "Well, it did. I have to make a gynecologist appointment next week for an ultrasound. You can come with me or you can't. Either way, I'll figure it out. I always do."

"Libby. I don't really know what to say right now. What do you want me to say? I'm kind of in shock."

And I was. I didn't expect to be a dad anytime soon. Hell, we hadn't been together that long and things were just starting to get good. Now...now...I didn't know what the hell was happening.

"Obviously you don't need to say anything. You're the first person I told. Now you should probably go so I can call my parents and tell them how I'm even more of a fuck up."

"Libby..." I pressed, trying not to make her angry. Hell, there was no way I would have wanted to face her dad and tell him I knocked up his baby girl.

"JUST GO!" She pointed at the door as she burst into tears.

I wanted to say something, anything. But my mind was in a fog.

I was going to be a dad. Shit.

"Okay. If that's what you want. I'll leave." I nodded and kept my head down, before standing up.

I should have kissed her, told her I loved her, and asked her to marry me or do something valiant, but instead I did what she asked and stood up, leaving her Aunt Dee's house and getting in my truck.

I drove to my mom's salon. She had a little place a block down from Dee's shop with a few other hair dressers. It was a small, shotgun style place with bright colored walls and tiled floors. There was a row of about five different stations and Mom's was at the back.

I walked past the row of women getting their hair yanked on, and ignored their stares as I made my way to my mom's station. "Hey, Ma, you got a minute?"

She looked at my reflection in the mirror in front of her. She was bent over one of the old church ladies, picking out her curly gray hair.

"Imma just finish Mrs. Raeger, then I can sit a spell if you want."

I nodded and swallowed. "Okay, I'll wait out front."

I didn't even wait for an acknowledgement. I just turned and headed out the front door and sat on the bench out front.

I'd quit smoking months ago, but I was craving the nicotine. My knee shook as I stared out onto the street. Across from me was the post office. A younger lady walked out with a little girl on her arm.

The little girl had blonde curls that bounced with each movement. Then she looked right at me and had the biggest, brightest blue eyes that I couldn't help but smile at.

I'd never really noticed kids before. Sure, I had nieces and nephews and I helped out with them, but now I'd actually created a child. Something that was mine.

"Is everything okay, Blaine?" Mom plopped down on the seat next to me.

She smelled like bleach and looked like hell with her hair pulled back. She pulled out a small mirror and ran her fingers over her face as if it was going to smooth out her wrinkles.

"Mama, I got something to tell you."

She closed her mirror and looked at me. "Don't tell me. Libby is pregnant and now y'all are going to run off to Vegas and get married."

She laughed when she said it, but when I winced she stared at me wide-eyed.

"Blaine, please tell me that none of that is true."

I rubbed the back of my neck. "Well, I haven't asked her to marry me...yet..."

Mom put her hands to her mouth and gasped. "She really is pregnant? I was just joking...I didn't...I mean...Is she going to keep it?"

I shrugged. "I guess so. I mean, I hope so."

"And you're really going to ask her to marry you now? Because you know you don't have to. Just because you have a baby with someone doesn't mean you need to marry them."

I shook my head and licked my lips. "I know, Mama. And it's crazy, but the more I think about it, the more I want this baby. I know it sounds nutty, but this is something I made. Something I've done with the girl I love more than anything. Hell, I love Libby more than I love college football."

Mom just shook her head. "This is not something I thought you'd be telling me today, Blaine Crabtree. Do her mommy and daddy know?"

I shook my head. "Not yet. But I'm assuming they will shortly."

"And do you think her daddy is going to say yes when you come a calling and asking for his daughter's hand?"

I let out a breath of air through my teeth. "I sure hope so."

Mom pulled me into a tight hug and I hugged her back because I didn't know what else to do. What else to say.

"Are you scared?" she whispered.

"Petrified."

"You know I'm here for you, baby, okay? If things start to go terribly wrong, or if you just need someone to talk to, I'll be here."

I pulled back and nodded. "I know, Mama. I just hope you and Dad won't be too disappointed."

"Are you disappointed?" she asked, staring at me wide-eyed

I rubbed the back of my neck and thought on it. "I'm disappointed that I didn't marry her before this happened, but I guess things just have to go a little bit out of order, so I guess I have to own up to it and put a ring on her finger."

"If that's what you want then I'll support you," Mom said, putting her hand on mine.

"Thanks, Ma, I appreciate you not freaking out."

She laughed. "Oh, trust me, darlin', I'm freaking out all right, but I'll save that for later. Right now, you need a mama to listen and tell you it's going to be okay, because it is. You just need to make sure you aren't going to break that little girl's heart again, because you know she may be carrying your little girl in there and you don't ever want to see somebody break your baby's heart."

I glanced back over across the street. The lady and the little girl were gone. It was just me and my mama. I turned back to her and nodded. "I'm not going to break her heart. I just hope she doesn't break mine."

I DIDN'T KNOW I WAS going there until I pulled up to Bubba Sinclair's place.

He was in the front of his shop, looking over an old Buick.

"Hey, Crabtree, haven't seen you in a while," he said in that thick Creole accent as soon as I jumped out of my truck.

"Yeah, I hadn't been needing any repairs for a while."

Bubba nodded, wiping his hands off on a towel. Bubba was a wide, pot-bellied man with a thick head of stringy hair, a permanent five o'clock shadow, and grease on just about every part of his tanned complexion. "Yeah, it's a mighty fine truck you got there."

I patted the hood of my truck. "It is. Which is why I'm hoping you could trade it for something else. Maybe a Blazer or something."

Bubba laughed. "Shit, son, you want to trade in this beautiful thing for some beat up SUV? Because I've got it, I'm just not sure you're going to like it."

I put my hands in my back pockets. "As long as it runs well, has air and heat, and will give me enough left over so that I can buy my girl a ring."

I'd remodeled an entire kitchen, put in new floors in the living room, used old cabinets to make nightstands, and even put together all the furniture in Mathieu's bedroom. But none of that could compare to trying to put together baby items.

I hunched over the plastic items in front of me and then stared at the directions. There was a picture of all the pieces, each labeled with a different letter. The second picture was the item half assembled. The third was a lady standing next to a happy baby in the little bouncer.

Nothing with how to actually put it together.

Libby leaned over me and put her arms on my shoulders. "How's it going?"

"I could probably build you one of these quicker with some wood scraps than I can figure out the directions to this thing." I held up the sheet of paper that could have been written in a different language and I still wouldn't have understood it.

Libby laughed, taking the paper and sitting down next to me. As the month was coming to a close, she was approaching her third trimester and definitely not as mobile as she used to be. Sitting down on the floor next to me looked like it was a huge struggle as she leaned back, moved her stomach, adjusting her shirt, and then finally sat with her legs straight out to the side of her, like a half-ass splits.

I raised an eyebrow. "You sure you're okay sitting down like that?

She rolled her eyes. "I'm not some kind of half-dead little girl. I can still move."

"I know. You just look uncomfortable."

"Well, there is a baby head that's poking my bladder and a baby foot that likes to kick my ribs."

I laughed. "So you're telling me that my boy is a fighter?"

She swatted my leg.

"Aw, I'm kidding, baby, come here." I held my arms out and she scooted closer until she was between my legs, resting her back on my chest. I put my arms around her and let my hands rest on her stomach.

"Does that feel any better?"

She nestled her head into my chest. "I think you're just doing this so you don't have to put together any more baby toys."

I picked up the directions and held them in front of us. "Naw, see, I can still work like this and now I've got two sets of eyes to help me read this damn thing."

"I don't think I'm going to be much help. To me that just looks like three different and weird pictures. The first is a bunch of junk. The second is half put together junk. The third is a creepy baby with a mom who looks like she wants to eat him for lunch."

I laughed at her assessment. "Hey, maybe that's how all mamas look at their babies when they're in this contraption."

"Do you really think I'm going to stare at Mathieu with my eyes wide and mouth open like that?"

"I've seen the way you look at bacon. You have that same face."

She pinched my side and I winced. "Hey, no need for that."

Libby looked up at me with a small smile on her lips. "You know you deserved that one."

I laughed and kissed her forehead. "Okay, you're right, I did."

Her smile fell slightly. "Do you think we're going to suck at this?"

I shook my head. "Baby, what makes you say that?"

She let out a deep breath. "I don't know. It's been a crazy year. We've gone from kind of hating each other, to being all over each other, to borderline hating each other again, then being all over each other and then BOOM, pregnant and wedding. Did you ever stop and think maybe we're being a little crazy here?"

I tilted her chin up to meet my eyes. "Libby Gentry, the moment I saw you at Jackson's parents' house, I knew there was something special about you. I wouldn't call it love at first sight, because that means I would have just fallen in love with your looks. But as soon as you opened your mouth and talked to me, I knew there was no going back. I may have stumbled and acted like an ass sometimes, but you've been there for me no matter what. You've taken me back during every single one of my stupid moments and supported me in some of the biggest changes we've had in our lives. I know that no matter what curveball life throws at us, that you're going to be here. When life feels like it's closing in the walls on me, you're there to rescue me. You're like the light in my darkness or something. I don't know, I'm getting pretty cheesy now. You can stop me anytime."

She giggled and bit down on her bottom lip. "No, it's not cheesy. It's sweet."

I brushed her hair from her face and then trailed my thumb down her jaw line and rested it on her chin before leaning in and pressing my lips to hers. Her hands moved up and fisted my hair as she deepened our kiss, her tongue sliding along my lips before her teeth slightly nibbled at my bottom lip, causing me to moan into her mouth. Damn the girl could kiss.

There was no urgency to get down her pants as soon as possible. No roaming hands. Just living in the moment of her sweet kiss and relishing in the feel of her body against mine.

When she broke the kiss, my body shuddered like I was missing something. Like my lips were supposed to be on hers forever. She gave me one last little kiss, then smiled. "If we keep kissing like that, we're never going to get this thing built."

I laughed and shook my head. "I don't know if it's going to get built anyway. Can you read these directions? Cuz I certainly have no idea what the hell is going on."

She patted my leg and then slowly pushed off of me until she was at a standing position. "How about I go and get my phone and we try and search for something online? Surely the Internet has some kind of trick for putting this together."

I raised my hands in the air. "Perfect! The Internet knows all!"

She smirked and waddled back toward the bedroom.

I leaned back over the different pieces of the toy and then stared at the directions again. "How the hell does this go together?"

I tried sticking the piece that I thought was A to B and nothing stuck. I tried another piece. Again. Nothing.

"Baby, where are you on those directions?" I yelled.

No answer.

"Baby?"

No answer again.

I dropped the pieces down and stood up then sauntered toward our bedroom. Libby was sitting on the bed, my phone in her hand as she stared down at it.

"Find those directions?" I asked, leaning against the doorframe.

She looked up at me, her eyes narrowed. "My phone was dead, so I went to charge it. Your phone was plugged in, so I unplugged it. That was when I saw a text flash across the screen. A text from someone named Julie. I thought, 'hmmm, maybe it's just some girl he works with asking about a work assignment'. Then I saw what she'd written, asking about coffee. I was curious, so of course I looked through the other texts."

My breath caught in my lungs and my mouth went completely dry. I'd been caught.

I could have said it was something innocent, but words failed me. I had no excuses.

She was off the bed and in three quick strides was over, shoving the phone in my face. "You've been texting your ex-girlfriend for almost a month while your pregnant wife has been working her ass off! When I think you've been going to work early, you're really having fancy coffee with her!" Her words came out between sobs as she beat my chest with her free hand. "How could you? After everything you just said to me! We're having a baby and you're banging your ex-girlfriend."

I took her hands, stopping them from their beating. "Hey, I'm not doing anything with Julie. I just happened to see her one day at the coffee shop near my job and talked with her a bit. She's been sending me some texts since then."

The tears streamed down Libby's face as she moved, trying to slam her tiny fists in my chest. "Yeah, texts that say she wished she wasn't sleeping alone! You're text flirting with her! And you've met her for coffee more than once! That's practically cheating. You're cheating on me, Blaine Crabtree!"

I swallowed hard. I never thought of it like that. Cheating to me was kissing or sleeping with someone else. It wasn't just about someone else taking my time.

But maybe Libby was right.

Still, I wasn't about to admit that to the hysterical pregnant woman.

"Baby. It's nothing. She means nothing."

Libby sobbed uncontrollably, her breath coming out shallow before she screamed and pulled back, grabbing onto her stomach and her body writing in pain.

"What's wrong, baby?" I reached for her but she pushed her hand out.

"Don't touch me. Don't you fu—" she screamed again, holding onto her stomach.

"Libby?" I whispered, slowly taking a step toward her with my hand out. I didn't know if she was about to attack me again, but the way her body slumped and she held onto her stomach, I knew something more was up.

"I think I need to go to the hospital. Mathieu may be coming," she yelled before she slumped to the ground, grabbing her stomach as she cried out in pain.

I'D NEVER DRIVEN SO fast in my life.

Libby didn't talk to me the entire way to the hospital. She just shook in pain with the occasional groans as she grabbed her stomach.

We still had eight and a half weeks before Mathieu was due. I thought we had more time to prepare.

I pulled into the hospital parking garage and offered Libby my hand to get out of the car, but she swatted it away and waddled past me.

I probably deserved that.

I followed her down the hallway until we got to the labor and delivery unit where she checked in and they brought us into a room.

I expected it to be a delivery room, but instead it was a smaller room with a few hospital chairs that looked like the ones they had in doctor's offices.

A younger looking nurse had Libby sit down on the table and then hooked a big band on her stomach that was connected to a machine. "We're just going to administer this non-stress test for a while and give your doctor a call. Since you're still almost nine weeks out from your due date this could just be Braxton Hicks or false contractions, but we'll continue monitoring you."

Libby nodded, then bit down on her bottom lip, withering in pain as the lines on the screen jumped and a ream of paper came out.

"Baby, I'm so sorry," I whispered, holding her hand.

Libby breathed in and out through her nose and closed her eyes before shaking her head. "I don't even know what to say to you right now, Blaine."

"Julie means nothing to me. I was stupid to even continue texting her or to meet up with her. I don't know why I did it, I guess I felt like maybe if she was coming after me then I didn't do anything wrong. That I was still a good guy."

Libby's eyes snapped open. "That doesn't make any sense. She cheated on you. You went home and slept with half the town, then met me, the girl who you said changed your ways, but it seems like old habits die hard."

I licked my lips. "I didn't do anything with Julie other than talk. I would never cheat on you. I love you."

She groaned, grabbing her stomach as her breathing quickened and the lines jumped on the screen.

Shit. This could really be happening. Mathieu could be coming.

I put my hands on her face and stood up, leaning over her. "Libby, listen to me. I love you. I've meant every damn word I've ever said to you. You're an amazing wife and you're going to be an even more amazing mother. I guess somewhere along the way I forgot what was important and it was stupid of me to let Julie text me. It won't happen again."

I pulled out my phone and deleted Julie's number along with all of her texts, something I should have done weeks ago. "She's gone. Never to return again. I promise."

Libby's brown eyes met mine, the fear in them evident as she shut them slightly, moaning and grabbing my wrists as the lines on the monitor jumped again.

For the next hour, we didn't say anything. We just stared at each other as I held onto her while she writhed in pain every few minutes.

Finally, Libby's doctor came in. She was a younger woman with curly red hair that she had pulled in a tight bun. I always wanted to ask Libby to ask for someone older, maybe more experienced, but she seemed to like this lady.

"Hey, Libby, how are we doing?"

"Not really that great," Libby muttered.

The doctor tore off the sheet of paper from the machine before unhooking Libby from it and sitting her up. Then the doctor took a wheeled stool across from her.

"When you first came in I thought these were just Braxton Hicks, or false contractions, but with these results, it does seem like they're the real thing. If you were at least thirty-six weeks I would just see where this would take us, but since you still have a ways to go, I'd like to give you something to stop the contractions, then put you on bed rest until we're closer to the due date."

"Bed rest? Like I have to lay in bed all day and do nothing?" Libby's eyes practically bugged out of her head.

"Or you can sit in a chair or anything else." The doctor pinched Libby's ankles, which were more like cankles now, the rest of her legs swollen like balloons. "Your body is swollen and I'm worried about what could happen if you were on your feet all day."

Libby looked up at me, tears falling down her cheeks. "What are we going to do?" she whimpered.

I put my arm around her and lightly pressed my lips to her temple. "We're going to do whatever we have to do, but we're going to get through this. You and me. Together."

BY THE TIME WE FINALLY got out of the hospital, it was dark. We weren't coming home with a baby, but with a lot of instructions that were going to severely limit Libby. She was going to call Dee about doing some work from home, but that was still going to be limited so she wouldn't deal with as much stress.

Her income wasn't much before, but now it was going to dwindle to almost nothing. The New Orleans job was paying me a hell of a lot more, but it was taking me away from Libby and I didn't want to put any more stress on her. I was the one who basically put her in this situation with my stupidity.

Neither of us said anything on the ride home and just listened to the radio. I wasn't paying too much attention to it until a familiar song came on. Our song.

I pulled over to the side of the road and turned up the sound.

"What are you doing?" Libby asked, raising her eyebrows.

I smiled and turned on the brights, hopping out of the car and running over to Libby's side to open the door.

"Blaine, what the hell are you doing?"

I gave her my hand. "Get out."

"Excuse me?"

"Come on, the songs almost over!"

She shook her head, but let me help her out of the car and I led her to the front of it. The music could still be heard softly and the headlights illuminated the cattails in front of us.

"What are you doing?"

I turned toward her, putting my arms around her waist as I pulled her close and swayed to the music. "It's our song, baby. The one we danced to at our wedding."

She put her arms around my neck and smiled slightly. "It is, isn't it?"

Libby leaned her head on my chest as we swayed to the music, not saying a word.

The future was so unknown for us. Mathieu could come at any time if we weren't careful. Libby's job was questionable and I was pretty sure she still hated me.

But in that moment, as I listened to the music and looked up at the stars, I closed my eyes and just felt her pressed against my heavily beating heart.

This was where I was supposed to be and I was going to make damn sure that nothing else would ruin it.

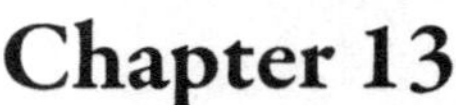

Chapter 13

I didn't want to leave Libby at home while I went to work.

My mom said she'd come over and help her out since it was her day off, but it was still hard to leave her, especially so early in the morning.

But I knew this was what I had to do.

Instead of taking the exit to New Orleans, I took the one before it and headed to The Roads and Highway department.

There were hardly any cars in the parking lot, but I knew it was open and that someone would be there for me to talk to.

The building wasn't anything special. It was a big, gray structure that sat in the middle of some other utility buildings. I would have missed it if it weren't for the big wooden sign out front that was squished between the one for the water department and the other one for waste management.

I parked my car and got out. The heat was already in the air, almost suffocating. The swampy air could melt paper it was so hot. I usually tried to put it in the back of my mind, but as I walked up the cement stairs and then entered the air conditioned building, I still couldn't stop sweating. I didn't know if it was the heat or just my nerves.

I walked down the fluorescent lit hallway and stopped at the main glass doors before opening them and stepping into the main area. There wasn't a front desk, just a lot of cubicles that were empty. But it was as if he knew I was coming. My former foreman, Daniel Vance, was sitting in his cubicle. I didn't know who else to talk to, but I thought he would be a good start.

"Blaine Crabtree, didn't expect to see you here," he said, standing up and giving me a brisk handshake.

I took a seat in one of the small gray chairs near his desk. "Yes, sir. I wasn't expecting this either, but I wasn't sure who else to talk to."

He sat in his chair and put his hands on his expansive stomach. "What can I help you with?"

I rubbed the back of my neck. I'd rehearsed this the entire way over in the car, but now that it was real, it was harder to spit out. "Well, sir, it was awfully nice of you to recommend me for the New Orleans job and I'm eternally grateful for it."

He raised his eyebrow. "Didn't think the work would be too hard for a fit guy like you, Crabtree."

I shook my head. "No, sir, it isn't that the work is too hard...but..."

I ran my hand over my face. This was harder than I thought, but I had to do it. "Sir, with a baby on the way, Libby needs me closer to home. I can take even the littlest, low man on the totem pole job as long as it means I'll be in Elsbury and able to leave at the drop of a hat if Libby needs me."

He nodded slowly. "As much as I hate to hear that, Crabtree. I can understand that. Family comes first."

I rubbed the back of my neck. "And, I'm going to need to cut my hours after this year. I've taken the assistant JV baseball coaching position at Elsbury and I'm going to try and go back to school. It won't be many hours to start, but I'm going to still be the best damn worker you've ever had whether it's five hours a day or fifteen."

He nodded, thinking on it a moment before he smiled slightly. "Well, Blaine, this wasn't the conversation I expected to be having with you, but I should have seen it coming. You're a bright man, almost too smart for your own good. I've always known you'd go onto greater things, but I'm happy to have you on the team in whatever capacity I can have you. You're going to be one hell of a hard guy to replace, though."

I licked my lips and nodded. "I know, sir, but if you don't mind, I think you should suggest Jackson Cleary for the job in New Orleans.

He's been doing this longer than me and is one hell of a worker. I can take over his pothole work and I'm sure he'd make a great addition to the team out there on the highway."

Daniel ran his fingers through his beard. "Jackson could be a good match for that. Thank you for the suggestion."

I nodded. "Thank you, sir."

Daniel put his hand on his desk. "I'll get the paperwork started. You'll have to still work in New Orleans today, but I'll get the word to your foreman and we should have you working on the Main Street potholes by tomorrow."

I grinned, not expecting to be that easy. "Thank you so much, sir. I promise that I won't let you down."

He took my hand, shaking it. "I don't doubt that at all, Crabtree."

BEFORE GOING TO THE site, I stopped at the coffee shop, knowing she'd be there.

And of course she was, sitting at the corner table with two coffee cups in front of her. The longer I'd been meeting up with Julie, the lower cut her blouses had become.

I don't know how I didn't see any of it coming or if I just chose to ignore it. But now I couldn't. Now it was time to do what was right.

"Hey, Blaine!" She smiled broadly and gave me a huge hug as soon as I approached the table. "I got you a coffee. Black, like you like it."

I nodded as she let go and sat down, but I didn't take the seat next to her. "I'm not staying, Julie."

"Oh, well, okay, maybe we can meet for lunch then?"

I shook my head. "No. We can't. We aren't going to keep doing this."

She blinked. "Doing what exactly?"

"Don't play dumb with me, Julie. I may have fallen for it before, but this has to stop. I'm married and you're the girl who cheated on me. I'm not saying I was a saint our entire relationship, but I never so much as talked to another woman. Libby loves me. She's having my son. She's never wronged me in any way and I've been one hell of an evil man, texting and having coffee with my ex-girlfriend."

She smiled, but it was forced. "We're just two friends having coffee and friendly conversation."

I shook my head. "You and I both know that this is more than that. I don't know exactly what it is, but it's going to stop. Your number is gone from my phone. No more contact between us, Julie. We may have history, but that history is going to stay in the past."

"Are you sure this is what you really want, Blaine?"

I took the drink and emptied it in the trash next to us. It was as if me dumping that was like dumping her. What I should have done before she went to college. What I should have done years ago when I was a shitty boyfriend and didn't know how to be a good one. It took a good long mess of years, but now I was finally figuring out what it took to be a good man. And being a good man meant that I had to get rid of all the old baggage.

"It is, Julie."

I didn't even look back at her or say goodbye as I turned and left the building, getting into my car and turning it on.

I waited a few minutes, hoping she didn't come running out, and thanking the Lord she didn't.

I pulled out my phone, seeing that I still had some time before I had to be on the site. I scrolled through my contacts until I found the right one and prayed the he answered.

"Dr. Gentry."

"Hey, Jack, it's Blaine."

"Hello, Blaine, I wasn't expecting your call. Libby called her mom last night, is everything okay? Do you need us to come down there?"

I winced and ran my hand over my face, trying to muster up the courage for what I needed to say. "Yeah. Everything's okay, but I need a favor."

"Okay."

"I'm cutting my hours at work and taking a job closer to home to help Libby out. With her not working as much, funds are tight. I'm going to be going back to school and Libby will be taking over the shop, so we'll have money, but for now..."

I let out a deep breath. God, I hated to ask anyone for anything.

"Let me guess, you need money?"

I sighed. "Let's call it a loan? I'll pay you back as soon as I can. We can even arrange a payment schedule. I hate to ask this sir, but I'm trying my best to do what's right for my family and I know that's going to require money. I can give your daughter all the love in me, but sometimes I'm not sure if it's enough."

He was silent a long moment before he finally responded. "Yeah, Blaine, I'll give you guys the loan. We can talk payment later. I'll get some money wired into Libby's bank account later today."

"Thank you, sir. I really appreciate it and I'll pay it back as soon as I can."

"Don't worry, Blaine. You just keep loving my daughter and grandson and the rest will follow."

I stared in the mirror. The same mirror that had been in my bedroom all of my life. Now I was leaving that bedroom forever. I made sure the last of my buttons were done and straightened out the brown suit jacket. I was thankful that Libby said wearing jeans and jackets were okay instead of stuffing myself into a tux. The last time I had to do that was senior prom and I vowed never to wear a damn bow tie or cummerbund again.

"Crabtree, stop checking yourself out. Do you think you're getting married or something?" Jackson smacked me on the back of the head.

"Yeah, I think something like that's going on." I turned around to where my groomsmen were gathered.

My brothers-in-law, Billy and Ronnie were sitting on my bed, passing a bottle of Jack back and forth. Don and Brian, Libby's brother-in-law, were in some sort of heated discussion about market research or some other boring business shit. Then there was Libby's best guy friend, Sawyer, who stood in the corner, staring out the window.

The first time I met Sawyer, I thought the redheaded string bean was just trying to bang my girlfriend. Then Libby told me that he was into men.

Truth be told, I'd never actually met a gay guy. Okay, maybe I had and just didn't know it, but there was still some big mystery to it. When she asked me if I'd take him as one of my groomsmen, she literally did it right before giving me a blow job, so there was no way I could say no.

She knew how to get me.

"Hey, Sawyer, you doing okay, man?" I walked over to the window and put my hand on his shoulder.

He barely looked back at me and ran his fingers through his overly gelled red hair. "Yeah, just watching them set up in the yard. Libby's mama is clucking like a mother hen and your mama is following close behind as they tell everyone where to put things."

I looked over his shoulder and saw just that: two blurs of purple dresses, wagging their fingers at men setting up different tables and flower arrangements.

I laughed and patted his shoulder again. "That is funny, but you know you don't have to stand over here in the corner. We're cool with you hanging out with us."

Sawyer turned toward me. "You don't have to pretend that you want me here, Blaine. I'm doing this for Libby because I love that girl like she's my sister and I know she wanted me to be a part of this."

I smiled. "Well, you and I at least have that in common. We both love that little blonde hurricane."

"You ready to meet that perfect storm at the end of the aisle today, Crabtree?" Sawyer asked, raising one of his very thin eyebrows.

I looked back to make sure the other guys weren't listening, then smiled at Sawyer. "I think I've been waiting for her all of my life."

THERE WAS ONLY ONE Catholic church in Elsbury and it was tiny, at least tiny compared to the mega church that Libby was used to in Chicago. But she wanted to get married here. I wanted to get married here. Elsbury was where we met and started our relationship and where I wanted to start our married lives.

That, and getting married in Chicago and those mega churches scared the shit out of me.

When her mama started talking about country clubs and big city things, I felt my insides go numb and thought I was going to purge.

But Libby wanted the small town wedding and reception in my parents' backyard as well. The big city girl had finally turned into my Southern belle. Well, at least somewhat.

As soon as I walked into the church, the scent of Magnolia blossoms hit me.

There were floral balls hanging from each one of the pews by silk hooks. Large arrangements of Magnolias sat along the priest's pulpit and covered just about every surface the white flowers could. A long burlap rug went down the center aisle, lined with Magnolia petals and the words 'Blaine & Libby' written in some fancy font at the end.

"Dayum, Crabtree, this is the fanciest I've ever seen the church," Jackson said, smacking my back.

I gulped and loosened my collar. This was almost too much. Too fancy. Too nice.

What the hell was I doing? I was going to give Libby this nice wedding then walk her into my moth ball smelling Meemaw's house and hope she'd say with me forever because I knocked her up in a janitor's closet.

Jackson followed the other groomsmen to the priest's office where we were to wait until the wedding started, but I couldn't move. My feet felt like they were stuck in wet cement and I just stared ahead.

"Blaine? Do you need some help? Your mama should be here soon," Sawyer said, coming to my side.

"Do you think Libby and I are doing the right thing?" I asked, not looking at him.

"Do you want my honest answer?"

I cocked an eyebrow and looked at him, but his gaze was straight ahead. "Yeah, give it to me, Blanchard."

He shook his head and smiled. "The day I met Libby, I immediately knew I wanted to be her best friend. There was something about the stylish girl and her contagious smile that I couldn't get enough of. That smiled broadened whenever she talked about you. Even when she was complaining, she was hiding that ghost of a smile."

He turned to fully face me. "If I could bottle up that little ball of sunshine and keep her smiling all the time I would. But I know you're the one that keeps that smile there and I'm pretty sure she keeps that smile on your face as well. She's not always happy, hell you're not always happy with her, and when you two fight it's like BAM, lighting." He put his fists together and pushed them out.

He continued, "But you always make up and her sunshine always comes back. Two people that collide in a perfect storm like you two, should hold on as tight as they can and enjoy every minute of it."

I grinned for the first time all day. "Thanks, Sawyer. That was what I needed."

He shook his head. "I just speak the truth, Crabtree."

THE CHURCH WAS PACKED. I think everyone in the entire parish was there for the wedding, even though we tried to keep it small. My hands

were shaking, so I shoved them in my pockets and couldn't even look up as the music started and the bridesmaids and groomsmen made their way down the aisle.

It wasn't until Canon in D played and I heard the shuffle of everyone rising that I finally looked up.

I choked back the lump in my throat seeing Libby at the end of the aisle. She wore a short white lacy dress that hugged her curves and instead of looking like a pregnant woman, she looked like one of those '50s bombshells they had in the old Hustlers. I'd be lying if I didn't say that, the dress hugging the curves of her hips and dipping low enough to give a hint of her tanned cleavage didn't do something for me.

Her long blonde hair fell in waves, framing her gorgeous face. She was biting her bottom lip as small tears fell from those big brown eyes. Instead of feeling turned on, I choked up and had to fight back my own tears.

I'm sure it would have been okay to cry at my own wedding and seeing my bride cry as she glided down the aisle, but I held it back and when my eyes met hers she finally smiled. And that was when I knew that there was no reason to be afraid anymore. There weren't any walls closing in on me. This was real. The girl walking toward me was my own perfect storm.

Chapter 14

I had to tell Libby that we took a loan from her parents. I wasn't sure how she would take it. On the one hand, I knew she wanted the nice things, but on the other I knew she would be spitting mad at me for even asking.

I wasn't even going to mention that I saw Julie.

The last thing we needed was for her to have a heart attack.

When I got home from work, I expected her to be in bed, like she was supposed to be. I walked into the bedroom and she wasn't there. The bed was made, another thing she wasn't supposed to do.

Shit. Was her car in the driveway? Was she so mad she took off?

"Libby?" I yelled, walking through the house.

"I'm in here!" her voice rang through the old walls.

"Where?"

"Mathieu's room."

I sauntered down the hallway to see her sitting on the floor with a pile of freshly washed baby clothes next to her. There was a little John Deere onesie already folded on her lap and she was mid-folding another one.

"What do you think you're doing?" I asked, shaking my head, crossing my arms, and leaning against the doorframe.

She looked up at me briefly then set the folded onesie to the side. "I'm sitting! The doctor said I didn't have to lay in bed all day."

I smirked and pushed off the door, walking the few feet over to her until I was sitting right in front of her and grabbed some clothes from the pile. "I don't think she meant that you should be doing laundry, though."

She rolled her eyes. "Oh, please. I'm fine. Really."

I set the folded shirt down and put my hand on hers, stopping her actions. Her brown eyes met mine as she bit down on her bottom lip and I knew she was anything but fine. Her feet were still swollen and a layer of sweat had formed on her forehead even though I was pretty sure the air was up as high as it could go.

"Why don't you have a seat in the rocker and let me finish this?"

She arched an eyebrow. "Are you sure? I don't think I've ever seen you fold clothes."

I smiled and stood up, helping her up as well. "A man has to change when it's necessary."

Putting my arm around her waist, I guided her over to the rocking chair and carefully helped her sit down. Once she was in place, I helped put her feet up on the ottoman and she folded her hands on her stomach.

"You know, a girl could get used to this."

I smiled. "All women should be treated like queens, not just when they're pregnant. I should be doing a better job of it."

I walked over to the already folded clothes and picked them up, walking to the dresser.

Libby pointed and yelled, "Top drawer for the newborns and 0-3 months. Second drawer for 3-6 months."

I laughed, shaking my head. "You make one hell of a queen and foreman."

She said something else, but I didn't hear her because my eyes zeroed in on something familiar in the corner. I put away the onesies and walked over to my old acoustic guitar, picking it up. Jackson helped me get it restrung before the wedding, but I hadn't played it since.

"What's this doing in here?" I asked, turning toward Libby.

She rocked gently. "I figured you may want to play some Cajun lullabies for Mathieu."

I laughed, slinging the guitar strap over my shoulder and strumming a few chords. "I'm not sure how many lullabies I know, especially Cajun ones."

She smiled. "That's what Google is for."

I strummed a few chords then hummed, walking toward her. "Hush, little baby, don't say a word..."

Libby smiled, slowly closing her eyes and she continued to rock.

I took a few steps closer until I was right in front of her, my hands continuing to strum the chords. "Papa's gonna buy you a mockingbird. If that mockingbird don't sing. Papa's gonna buy you a diamond ring."

"I knew you'd know some lullabies," Libby said, keeping her eyes closed.

I sat down on the floor next to her and leaned over, kissing her stomach, then went back to strumming. "If that diamond ring turns brass. Papa's gonna buy you a looking glass."

I'd felt Mathieu move a few times and seen him move when we were in the hospital, but this was the first time I really watched him roll across Libby's stomach as if he were trying to get situated and settle down for slumber.

I smiled, watching him in awe.

"He liked it," Libby whispered, "keep going".

I picked a few more chords and wet my lips. "If that looking glass gets broke, Papa's gonna buy you a Billy goat."

Mathieu rolled a few more times then he settled on the left side of Libby's tummy, the closest to me, as if he was finally settling and wanted to listen to more.

"If that Billy goat don't pull, Papa's gonna buy you a cart and bull."

I kept playing and singing. The last time I'd done either was at our wedding, a surprise to Libby, that Jackson and I planned. She'd asked me why I hadn't played in a while and it was really because I didn't have the time between work and wedding planning. Now I was finding I had even less time for things, but seeing the smile on Libby's face even as she drifted off to sleep, I knew I'd have to do more of it.

I strummed the last few chords and sang, "You'll still be the sweetest little baby in town."

I set down my guitar and leaned over, kissing Libby's forehead, then kissed her stomach softly. "Goodnight, Mathieu. I can't wait to meet you, but you can stay in there as long as you need to."

Libby was the first girl I'd brought home to meet my parents.

I guess technically it was Julie, but they already knew her from us growing up together.

To say I was nervous was an understatement.

Libby had been moody the past few days, ignoring me with dumb excuses. It made me think she really didn't want to meet my parents. Maybe she didn't think I was good enough for her and I was just the Southern boy that was taking her mind off of things.

The moment I saw her in her room, laughing with that tight purple dress, I couldn't help but smile. She was too damn pretty for her own good and I knew I was falling way too hard for her.

We pulled up to my parents' house and I could already see Abby staring out the window. I knew it would only be a few minutes before the little girl ran out. She would probably be followed by Meg and Alicia, my too-crazy-for-their-own-good sisters. Damn, I was nervous. This prim and proper city girl was going to meet my family. The ones who didn't have any chairs or plates that matched and liked to yell in the middle of dinner.

"Do you think they're actually going to like me?"

I glanced over at Libby, raising an eyebrow. I wasn't expecting those to be the words that came out of her mouth. I didn't think she'd be the one who was nervous. Was this why she was being so cold? "Do you think you're going to stop ignoring me like you have been?"

She turned toward me, tilting her head slightly which just made her even more adorable. "What?"

"Libby, you've been ignoring me for days now, with the lamest excuses. Headaches, Jeopardy, and I just want to know what's going on." I cupped her face in my hands and pulled her closer. The smell of her shampoo and perfume surrounded me, she always smelled amazing and it was hard for me to think of anything, let alone keep myself from getting turned on, but I had to focus. I couldn't keep doing this if it was just her summer fling.

"If you are going to break up with me, please just tell me now, so I don't have to introduce you to my parents. Then have my crazy sister, Meg, try and put a curse on you or something."

She giggled, but I kept my focus on her. "I'm serious, Libby."

"Well, are you breaking up with me?" Her eyes softened

"What? Libby why would you even think that? You know I'm crazy about you." I blinked hard and put my hands down, unbuckling my seatbelt so I could get closer to her. I didn't know what was going on through her pretty little head. Did she think I was some manwhore? She'd told me about her ex cheating and I didn't want her to think the same of me.

"Yeah, but how many other girls have you told that to? I mean, UGH. I don't know what to think! I think I probably think too much." She slumped down, putting her head in her hands.

"Libby." I tugged on her waist and pulled her closer to me, tilting her chin up so those chocolate brown eyes met mine. "Look, I care about you, and just stop thinking about your ex. I'm not like him. The past is all you have with him, and the past, is the past the future is now."

She smiled. "Did you just quote Christopher Walken?"

"Yes. Yes I did. Does it do anything for you?" I pressed my forehead to hers.

"Oh yeah." She leaned into kiss me lightly, but I took that chance to pull her closer and when she parted her lips, letting her tongue meet mine, I couldn't help but smile under the kiss. This girl was definitely something and I intended to keep her around.

Shortly after, of course, my niece interrupted our kiss and it was time to meet my family.

I tried not to cringe when Meg hugged her way too tight and when Mom and Meg laughed at Libby for practically throwing the pie at them that Dee made.

When Mom suggested that I show Libby around, I let out a sigh of relief. It would be good to give her a tiny break from the family.

I didn't want to think about what was going through her head as she saw my parents' tiny house. I just kept talking it up like it was the greatest place ever. Maybe she didn't see it, but I saw years of memories. The house that built me.

I led her up to my bedroom, which was originally the attic that Dad and I had refinished. I had a real sense of pride in my first big carpentry project. Her eyes roamed around the wooden planks and I saw her wince when she had to duck in some areas. But I did find her staring longingly at the bed before she picked up the picture I had on my nightstand.

It was my favorite picture of us. It may not have been the best. Her face was scrunched as she laughed and mine was all puckered up from kissing her forehead. But I liked it. It showed both our personalities. Maybe it was cheesy to frame it.

Shit. Maybe I should have removed it.

"Really Blaine?" She leaned against the dresser across from my bed. "Out of all the pictures we have from my phone and that I put on Facebook, and you picked this one?"

I shrugged, trying to be nonchalant and not act like I spent hours looking through Facebook and then sent it to Wal-Mart to get printed. "I like that one."

She rolled her eyes, but then stopped and set down the picture. She walked over to the corner, picking up my guitar before she spun toward me. "Do you actually play?"

I grinned, slowly walking toward her. Dad had started me playing when I was just a little thing, sitting on the front porch, strumming the chords to "Smoke on the water". "Of course I play. Did you think I just keep it around for decoration?"

"How about you play me something then?" She raised her eyebrows and that smile broadened.

"Well...Then I'd have to take it from you." I took the guitar and slung the strap over my shoulders.

"I don't mind." She sat down on my bed, the hem of her skirt inching up to show off those long, tanned legs. Damn if it wasn't the sexiest thing I'd ever seen.

"Well what do you want to hear?" I had to swallow hard and readjust myself under the guitar before I walked over and sat down next to her.

"Surprise me." She leaned back so she was propped up on her elbows, giving me an even better view of those legs. My eyes followed up her dress until I was at her smile, then staring into those chocolate brown eyes.

Before I even knew what I was doing, I was strumming along and singing "Brown Eyed Girl." Her eyes widened before she smiled, tapping her foot along to the song.

I liked singing and playing guitar, but watching Libby actually enjoy it, made me love it even more.

When the song was done, I leaned forward and whispered, "You are my brown eyed girl."

Then I kissed her. I wanted all of her on my bed right then and there. I had to stop briefly just to put my guitar down, but then I was right back to her lips.

Her fingers trailed down my stomach and soon, they were pulling my belt through the loops.

I wanted her. I wanted her so damn bad, but I had to stop. For one, I wasn't about to do it with my parents right downstairs. And for two, she meant more to me than a random conquest. If I gave in now, all it would be was sex. I didn't want that for either of us.

I pulled away and sat up. A few more seconds and I knew I'd give in.

Of course this pissed her off and she laid on the bed, letting out a deep breath and yelling "ugh!" Dammit if that didn't make it worse with her skirt going up those thighs, giving me a peek at her lacy pink panties.

"I don't think we are ever going to do anything!" She put her hands over her eyes and sighed. "You know, for being this big playboy that everyone talked about, you sure are acting like Hugh Hefner without any Viagra."

I crawled next to her then hovered over her, trying not to press myself against her or she'd know how turned on I was and I'd be a goner. "Libby, I couldn't be more attracted to you."

"Then why haven't you even tried anything more than making out with me?" She pouted out that bottom lip and I just wanted to kiss her.

"Libby... You're not like other girls I've dated. I want more than just to screw you. And believe me I do want to do that, BAD." I kissed a trail down her neck and collarbone until I was kneeling on the floor between her legs and kissing a line up her thighs, her body quivering beneath my lips.

She looked down at me through hooded lashes, "You don't have another girl on the side."

"Libby, baby, I don't think I could ever have another girl besides you."

Chapter 15

Bed rest for Libby was hard on all of us.

Or maybe it was just me.

She was able to work from home a bit on her computer, but that didn't stop her from being bored.

And when she was bored, she did online shopping.

I guess not all of it was bad, she did get us a sectional couch with recliners for a steal, but now she spent most of her time on the recliner, surfing the Internet for more deals.

I sat down next to her on the new couch. It still smelled like new, clean fabric.

"Working hard, baby?"

I just got off working down on Main Street. It was seriously a lot of piddly stuff. I would have complained about it, but I was still getting paid, and I was able to get off in time to spend the late afternoon with Libby without a long drive.

I stared at her computer screen where one of those baby boutiques was pulled up.

"Do you really think that Mathieu needs more clothes? Didn't I just put away an entire dresser full?" I raised my eyebrows.

"But now that we have the extra money and there is a sale...I thought we could get him ready for next season." She bit down on her bottom lip, keeping her eyes on the computer screen.

I shook my head and set her computer down on the coffee table. Another new purchase online, that I had to put together.

"Baby, I know we got the loan from your parents, but we can't keep spending all of this money all willy nilly."

She laughed and shook her head. "Who the hell says willy nilly?"

I stared at her, not breaking my glare. "Don't change the subject."

She narrowed her eyes. "Geez, way to be a dick."

"Now, baby, don't be like that. I'm trying. I'm trying real hard to support us, and it sucks that I had to get this loan, but I plan on paying every penny back to your dad, and I can't do that if we're spending everything in our account."

She blew out a big puff of air but said nothing.

"Hey..." I tilted her chin, forcing her eyes to mine. "Look, I'm not trying to be a dick. I'm really not. I just really want to be able to do this. Your dad put a lot of money in our account, more than I could ever dream of having. I took a big pay cut by leaving the New Orleans job, but I did it for our family and I'd do it again in a heartbeat. I just...I don't want this all to be for nothing."

She tilted her head slightly. "Do you think I don't appreciate all that you're doing?"

I shrugged, leaning back. "Sometimes. I know I sound like a girl and all, but yeah. I work my ass off every day and I've been coming home to more furniture on our porch or you sleeping. I know, I need to get over it. You're carrying my baby and you're on bed rest, but it still gets to me."

She smiled softly and put her hand on mine. "I'm sorry, Blaine. I do appreciate you working so hard. I guess I just got carried away now that we had money again."

She sighed. "But, really, I guess money isn't everything. Sometimes I forget that. I grew up never wanting for anything, never knowing struggle. It shaped me into something I didn't like. A spoiled princess that I was when I first moved her...but I think meeting you helped to change that."

"You weren't a spoiled princess, baby. Maybe a little high and mighty, but not a spoiled princess."

She laughed. "Don't try and get on my good side. Your damage is already done."

I put my hands up. "Hey, now, I'm just being honest."

She sighed. "And I guess I've been acting like that high and mighty princess again lately. I'll blame the hormones and our bank account. I'll keep it in check from now on, okay?"

I smiled, shaking my head. "Not sure I believe you, but you can try."

"Okay, fine, I'll try. Is that better?"

I leaned in and kissed her lightly. "Trying is all I can ask for."

Me: Kristi, I know you don't know me from Adam, but this is Blaine Crabtree. Libby's boyfriend, or possibly ex-boyfriend. Look, I know it's your wedding and you probably hate me and all, but I want to make everything up to Libby and I need your help.

I stared at the computer screen before I clicked 'send' and sent the message.

It was the only life line I had. I had to try and make things right. After the phone call from Libby and hearing her words, I knew I had to. Her voice was so hurt. So painful. I wanted to do anything I could to make it better.

Just telling her I loved her over the phone wasn't going to cut it. I had to show her.

"I may be angry. I may be hurt. But, undeniably I am still in love."

Those words haunted my dreams and I couldn't sleep, so I sent the message to Kristi and prayed.

I half-way didn't expect a response, and half-way expected if there was one, then she'd be swearing at me.

But just like that, she messaged me back.

Kristi: Your plans better involve a lot of roses and groveling.

I shook my head and smiled for the first time all day.

Me: Maybe. I also think I need to get my way to Chicago. I've never actually flown before and have no idea what the hell I'm doing.

It took a while before Kristi messaged me back and when she did it was a bunch of different links.

Me: What the hell are all of these for?

Kristi: Don't get sassy. These are sites to book plane tickets and rental cars. It won't be cheap, I can tell you that much, since it's only a few days away. I really hope you can pull this off. I'm actually rooting for you.

Me: What does that mean?

Kristi: It means you need to get your ass on a plane and make my little sister feel better.

I cringed, pulling out my debit card and booking the flight and car rental. I hadn't spent that much money since I bought my truck.

I wouldn't have had to spend the money if I wasn't a dick and just went with Libby in the first place, but now I was really going to do this. I was going to make the biggest step I'd made in my life at that point.

I clicked okay and bought the tickets, praying that she'd still have me.

THE FLIGHT TO CHICAGO was my first flight ever. I never had the need to go anywhere. We didn't do much for vacation other than go to the coast, and one time to Texas for the rodeo. Mom and Dad weren't exactly wealthy and three kids were expensive.

The piece of paper was burning a hole in my suit pocket. If just offering Libby to come back with my love didn't work, I had another plan.

It was selfish, sure. She probably wanted to get back to her college in Illinois, but I had to give it a shot. Her parents probably already hated the boy that broke her heart and one little piece of paper wasn't going to make it better. But I'd done my research. I'd looked up all that I could about her credits transferring to St. Joseph Community College and what the drive would be like. I'd done so much damn research I thought about going there myself.

But not now. This wasn't my time. This was hers.

I watched the Chicago skyline come into view and sucked in a deep breath. Even from a distance, it exuded all the things I didn't have: class, structure, and wealth. Seeing it made me wonder if I was still doing the right thing. Maybe Libby was already ready to move on and realize that she was just slumming it with me.

I prayed hard that she hadn't.

I had to catch a later flight, so I missed the wedding completely. I had to haul ass, changing into my suit and getting into the tiny rental car to make it the hour out to the suburbs.

The resort on Lake Michigan looked like something out of a magazine with its pretty brick exterior and large white columns. That wasn't half as nice as the moonlit path that trailed out to the beach where tiny, twinkling lights hung above a crowd of people.

I put my hands in my pockets, sauntering down the path and trying to act casual, but I was sweating bullets.

What the hell was I doing?

I didn't have any sort of plan or even know if I was at the right wedding. I could have walked in just to have someone escort me out, or worse, see Libby in the arms of another man.

I turned to leave, ready to go back to the rental car and just text Libby, but a hand caught my elbow. I turned around to see a small redhead wearing a very poufy white dress. "Blaine?"

I nodded. "You must be Kristi?"

She smiled. "Well, I'm glad you showed up, cowboy, someone has been waiting for you."

I looked behind her, scanning the crowd, but I didn't see Libby.

She crooked her finger. "Follow me."

I walked past the staring and whispering crowd and followed Kristi down to the beach. That was when I saw her. Libby was sitting alone, the moonlight casting shadows on her long blonde hair. I couldn't see her face and I knew as soon as I did, I'd be a goner.

Even if she turned me down. Even if she never wanted to see me again, I had to tell her that I loved her. That she meant more to me than a summer fling. That Libby Gentry was my forever and I wasn't going to run away ever again.

Chapter 16

The weeks felt like they were taking eternity. All I did was work and come home and take care of the house and Libby. It was exhausting, not to mention, with bed rest, we also weren't allowed any kind of intimacy. Nothing. I thought maybe I could get a little action below my belt, but Libby would just whine about how uncomfortable she was and that was an instant mood killer

So, I had to resort to my own devices.

"Hey, babe, I'm going to be in the bathroom for a while."

"Ew, I don't want to know about your pooping habits." Dina sat on the couch next to Libby. Some reality TV show was on, but Libby was looking from the TV to her computer.

After our talk, she had curbed her online shopping habit, but with Dina now going in on the business with her, they were both making plans. I never thought I'd see the girl work as hard, but she was always pulling up spreadsheets and looking at other similar companies' business models.

I hated to admit that it was kind of a turn on to see a hard-working woman.

A lot of her friends and my family members had been coming by to help us out with dinner and whatever chores needed done. I was working less since I was doing piddly jobs in Elsbury, but that didn't stop people from coming by.

People were always over. Sometimes a man just needed his privacy.

"I'll make sure I'm extra loud with the fart noises for you, Dina." I winked and grabbed a magazine from the coffee table for good measure before I sauntered into the bedroom.

Finally, I could be alone, and when I closed my eyes, I could think about another time. Before babies. Before married life.

Libby giggled, covering her mouth.

Damn, I should have known the little glowing candles would be too much. I'd never tried so damn hard for a girl, but there was something special about her. Something that I knew deserved more than throwing her down in the back of my truck and jack hammering her.

"What? Too much?" I put my arms out as if I was encompassing the entire room.

"It is a little cheesy." She laughed again, removing her hand from her mouth.

"Dangit. I just wanted to do something...to make it you know...special and what not." I dropped my hands and took a few steps toward her.

She bit down on her bottom lip and looked at the floor. I knew I was a goner right there looking at the sweetest little thing in the glow of the candlelight. "Are you sure?"

I lifted her chin so that her eyes met mine. They were slightly hooded and I had to bite my tongue to stop from just telling her how bad I wanted her. If she would have told me 'no', I'd have to excuse myself to the bathroom and get it all out. "Libby, I'm not going to do anything you don't want to do."

I took her hand and led her further into my bedroom. It was about time I explained myself instead of running like I always did. "When I wouldn't sleep with you at Jackson's, it wasn't because I didn't want to. Trust me, I did." I smiled, blowing a breath of air out of my nose.

"I just wasn't going to have it be some meaningless thing, just throwing you down on someone else's waterbed at a party. You are definitely too good for that, and I wanted to make sure that is not how you remembered the first time we did it."

I meant it. Every damn word. She deserved more. Hell, she probably deserved better than me, but there was something about her. Something special. She was perfect, even her flaws made her that much more perfect to me.

I took another step closer and peeled my shirt off, throwing it to the side. I hadn't worked out much, but manual labor more than made up for that. I could tell she appreciated it by the way her eyes roamed over my body.

"Joie De Vivre?" she questioned, putting her arm around my waist and pressing that tight little body against me.

"Zhwah duh viv-re," I said in my best French accen,. "It means the joy of living."

She looked up at me, unhooking her lip from her teeth before she grinned. "Then let's enjoy."

She kissed me hard and that was all I needed to pull her closer and let a little sigh escape her lips. I growled, deepening our kiss and wanting all of her as soon as possible.

"I didn't wear the lingerie, so I hope you aren't too disappointed," she whispered as I trailed a line of kisses down her neck to her collarbone.

Her body trembled as I slowly pulled off her little jacket and tank top. Damn she was beautiful. She was all tanned skin. My eyes trailed down to her belly ring and the curve of her hips that dipped into her shorts that I wanted my hands in so damn badly.

"You know baby, we don't have to do anything you don't want to do...We can still play Duck Hunt..." I leaned in and placed feather light kisses on her collarbone, barely touching her, but letting my breath trail over her skin.

She pulled on my belt loops and pressed me against her. I grinned, taking the chance to unhook her bra and let it fall to the ground. Her small, perfectly rounded breast pressed against my chest and I was about to burst out of my boxers.

We walked slowly toward the bed, peeling off my pants on the way there. Once we go to the bed, Libby laid down and slowly I pulled down her pants and those little white panties. She was even more perfect, naked, in all her glistening glory.

I kissed down her legs and then back up before reaching for my boxers. But before I could she put her hand on the top of my waistband.

"Wait," she whispered.

"Do you really want to stop right now?" I was practically falling out of my boxers and with her laying on my bed, spread out, there was no way I could stop.

"No." She ran her tongue over her bottom lip and if I wasn't already hard as a rock, I was now even harder.

"But...um do you...you know have something? You know a wrap it before you tap it?"

God damn, she was cute as hell. Her cheeks flushed as she hooked her bottom lip in her teeth again.

I couldn't help but laugh. "You mean a condom, Libby?"

"Yeah."

I didn't say a word, I reached over to my nightstand and grabbed a gold foil package from the fresh pack I bought, hoping I'd get to use it with her.

"Do you want to do it?" I asked.

"Ew!" She scrunched her face and if at all possible, she looked even cuter.

"Really Libby?" I raised an eyebrow.

She sighed. "Blaine, please just do me already."

I slid the condom on, tossing the wrapper to the side. Splaying my hands on either side of her waist, she immediately hooked her legs around my middle and her eyes rolled back as I slowly slid in, filling her completely.

If there was a heaven, I was pretty sure that's what Libby felt like.

"Blaine? Are you...OH MY GOD!"

I didn't hear the door, but I heard Dina's voice loud and clear as she caught me with my pants down, literally seconds from finishing.

Quickly, I pulled them up, zipping, and fastening my belt. "Dina, don't you knock?"

She covered her eyes. "I didn't see anything!"

I shook my head, all the blood rushing from my pants up to my face. I wasn't the guy who got embarrassed, but damn, I'd just got caught masturbating in my own bedroom. At least she didn't know it was because I was thinking of the first time with my wife.

Hell, she didn't need to know that or that I masturbated.

"Um, you have a visitor. She's in the kitchen." Dina kept her eyes covered as I walked out of the bedroom.

"She?"

Dina nodded.

"Hey Dina?" I asked.

"Yeah?"

"Can we not tell anyone about this?"

Dina laughed. "I'd be too embarrassed to ever bring it up."

I nodded. "Good. Now I guess I should see who my guest is."

I walked down the hall with Dina following behind me and she practically ran into me when I stopped and stared at the blonde haired girl in my kitchen.

"Nikki? What are you doing here?"

Libby sat at the kitchen table. "I asked the same thing."

Nikki put her hands out. She was leaning on the counter with four large foil trays in front of her. "Now, don't get mad at me. I thought this might be sort of a peace offering. My older sister, Tammy, and I wanted to help y'all out and made some freezer meals so y'all wouldn't have to worry about the cooking. These should last you at least a couple days and the directions are on them."

I rubbed the back of my neck. "Well, that was awfully nice of the two of you."

Nikki sighed. "It's about time I did something nice. I've been a real bitch. I mean, what the hell kind of girl gets drunk and starts yelling nonsense at a wedding? Not the kind of girl that I want to be."

"Yeah, it wasn't one of your finest moments," Libby muttered.

Nikki frowned. "I'm sorry, to both of you. For everything. I know that this isn't going to make up for it right now, but I'm going to keep trying. Blaine has been friends with me and my family since we were all running around in diapers. I should have never let my little crush get in the way of that and I did. I become a crazy girl because of it."

Libby smiled. "Sometimes we do crazy things for the boys we like."

I looked between the two girls. "So, does this mean we're all cool now?"

Libby stood up slowly and waddled over to the counter, examining the foil containers. "No, but I think that this Cajun chicken pasta may be a good start."

Chapter 17

Even when we don't want it to, life moves and sometimes life moves too quickly.

August had gone by in no time and things were slowing down even more at work.

Libby was done with school and spent her time getting things ready for the baby. She was still on bed rest, but that didn't stop her from sneaking away to fold some baby clothes or try and put together whatever toy she could.

I finally gave in to getting her out of the house when Jackson and Dina said they were hosting a Labor Day barbecue.

I still wasn't able to look Dina in the eye since she caught me with my pants down, but she was Libby's best friend and I had a feeling the two were going to make the announcement soon that they were taking over Dee's shop.

"Is it lame if my dish to pass is a Jello-O salad that Nikki made?" Libby asked as she finally got out of the car.

Her poor body was so swollen that it was like hell for her to get in and out of the car. Her face may have been puffy and there may have been dark circles under her eyes but nothing could stop her beautiful smile. Sawyer really was right, she was a ball of sunshine.

I shook my head, letting her hook her arm through mine. "Naw, I think Nikki will appreciate you sharing."

"Is she going to be here today?" Libby asked.

"I assumed so. You talk to her more than I do."

She laughed. "Only because I think that girl thinks that feeding me and bringing me baby clothes is going to win my heart."

I arched an eyebrow. "Is it working?"

"A little."

We went around the back of Jackson and Dina's place where the party was already in full swing. Jackson was behind his new giant grill and Dina was at the bar, but they both stopped what they were doing as soon as we walked in.

"The Crabtrees have finally left their house!" Jackson yelled, cupping his hands together.

Everyone parked in their chairs raised their glasses and let out a "whoop".

Jackson put his arm around Libby and helped guide her to an empty chair. "And now that they're here, I have an announcement to make, well more like Dina and Libby do."

Libby looked from me to Dina and then back again. All eyes were on them.

Libby slowly stood up from her chair and then made her way to stand next to Dina. "Well...should I tell them or should you tell them?" Libby asked.

"Just tell us!" Butch Sinclair yelled.

Libby rolled her eyes. "Okay, fine! Dina and I are going to be partners."

"Y'all are getting hitched?" Butch asked.

Dina threw an empty beer can in Butch's direction and he ducked before it hit him. "No, stupid, business partners! We are taking over Dee's shop!"

Everyone clapped and let out another "whoop".

"Now it won't be for another few years, but slowly you're going to see some changes and I think you guys are going to love it," Libby said, the smile plastered on her face.

Jackson sauntered over the girls, but his eyes were on Dina. "Yeah, there are some mighty big changes happening around here. Blaine and Libby are having a baby. Libby and Dina becoming business owners..."

Slowly Jackson bent down until he was on one knee and then pulled out a small black box that he opened to reveal a sparkling diamond ring. "And I'm hoping that Dina agrees to be my wife."

Dina practically tackled him with tears in her eyes. At some point I'm guessing she said yes because Jackson started hooting and hollering and picked her up, throwing his fist in the air.

With all the commotion and people congratulating, I lost Libby in the crowd. But when I found her, I knew something wasn't right.

Her hand was on her stomach and she leaned against one of the chairs as Nikki hovered over her, smiling and carrying on.

"Excuse me, Nik, I need a moment with my wife," I said, pulling Libby away.

"Are you okay?" I asked.

Libby winced. "No. I don't think I am."

My eyes widened. "Are you? Is this?"

Her face wrinkled again and I held onto her as she breathed heavily and then sighed, leaning against my chest. "I think it's time to go to the hospital. I think Mathieu is ready to make his debut."

I SPED LIKE HELL TO the hospital, not giving a lick about the holiday traffic.

As soon as we got to the emergency room, a nurse came with a wheelchair and got us back to a room.

Libby held onto my hand, practically crushing it every time she would writhe in pain.

"It's going to be okay, baby. Breathe!"

"YOU BREATHE!" she yelled as she laid back on the hospital bed.

The wide-eyed nurse stood at the foot of the bed. "Okay, Libby, I'm just going to check you to see if you're dilated."

The woman slipped her hand under Libby's gown. "Now you're going to feel some pressure."

Libby clenched her hand onto mine and I swore that she turned it white.

The woman was down there an awfully long time, I thought, before she finally pulled a gloved hand out. "You're about five centimeters."

I looked from the nurse to Libby. "What does that mean?"

"You have to be at ten to deliver," Libby said.

The nurse smiled. "It means that you're going to be a daddy."

A GUY IN SCRUBS CAME in and shot a needle in Libby's back for an epidural. They said it might slow down the process of her dilating, but it would take away some of the pain.

It didn't slow down shit.

Another nurse came in a few minutes later and Libby was still writhing in pain. "I feel like I need to take the biggest poop ever," Libby whined and I tried not to laugh.

"Well, let's just see if anything is moving along," the nurse said, putting her hand under Libby's gown again. All these nurses were getting more action than I was.

The nurse pulled her hand out and then put it on Libby's knee. "I'm going to go find your doctor. It's time to push."

Libby's eyes widened. "What? Really?"

"I'd better go call my mama and yours," I said and tried to pull away, but Libby locked a death grip on my hand.

"NO, you're not leaving me right now. I need you!"

I looked down at her big brown eyes and her trembling lip. This was it. The moment we'd been waiting for these last few months. She was right. I couldn't leave her now.

A lady came in wheeling some little cart with a light on it, followed by Libby's doctor in scrubs.

"Okay, Libby, are you ready for this?" she asked.

Libby shook her head. "No, but I guess I have to be."

Two nurses put Libby's legs in stirrups.

"Okay, Daddy, I'm going to need you to stand where you are and help hold her leg. Now, Libby, tell me when you feel a contraction and then your husband is going to count to ten with me and you're going to push for ten. Then stop. When you feel another one we'll do the same thing."

"I FEEL IT, I FEEL IT!" Libby screamed.

"Okay, let's push!" the doctor said.

I counted as Libby's body shook and her face scrunched up. We did this, what seemed like a hundred times, and nothing moved.

"Maybe we could take a little break and come back. Your body might not be ready," the doctor said.

"Like hell," I replied and looked down at Libby, smoothing her sweaty hair from her face.

"Baby, you've got this."

She shook her head, tears springing from her face. "No, I don't. It's too hard. I should just let them do a C-section."

I put my hand on her chin and forced her to look at me. "Nothing is too hard for my girl. You've gotten through college, survived marrying me, and you're about to own your own business all while being a new mama. You're the strongest woman I've ever met and it's why I love you. It's also why I know you can do this. I'm going to be right here every step of the way."

She let out a big breath and nodded. "Okay. I'll try."

"That's my girl." I kissed her forehead, then moved back.

"Okay, I feel another contraction," Libby said weakly.

Then with her legs pulled back she yelled, scrunching her face as the doctor counted.

"That was a great one, Libby. A couple more of those and I think your baby's birthday is going to be today."

I squeezed her hand. "Come on, Mama, you can do this."

She pushed again and within a few more pushes, I heard the most glorious sound in the world, Mathieu's cry.

The doctor laid him on Libby's chest as I cut the umbilical cord, but I could barely take my eyes off of him. He had soft white hair and the bluest eyes I'd ever seen. Bluer than mine. His skin was tanned and everything about him was more perfect than I could have ever imagined.

I thought I fell in love with Libby the moment I first spoke to her, but I fell even more in love with her the moment I saw her holding our son.

"Do you want to hold him, too, Daddy?" Libby asked, looking up at me.

I smiled. "Of course."

I took Mathieu in my arms. I knew I only had a few moments before the nurses would whisk him away to clean him up and do whatever tests they had to do. But in that moment, looking into my sons eyes, I didn't think about the future, or what else the crazy world had to offer. I just knew that this was my family. This was my happiness.

Epilogue

Five Years Later
Libby

Sleeping was never easy. But sleeping was especially hard when Mathieu was crammed in between Blaine and I in bed, and three-year-old Carter was working his way up to tackle Blaine.

I watched out of the corner of my eye as the little curly haired blond approached him like a tiger, then pounced on his unsuspecting and sleeping father.

"Ow!" Blaine rolled over, exposing his tanned chest. Even though his road crew days were coming to a close, that man still knew how to keep his body looking great.

I, on the other hand, at twenty weeks pregnant with our third child, and hopefully our last since she was a girl, was not looking so hot.

"Carter, what do you think you're doing?" Blaine asked, sitting up with Carter promptly standing on the bed next to him.

"It's mommy's big day! We're going to eat cake and try not to break anything."

Blaine laughed. "I take it you told them that there are still breakables at the shop?"

"You know it." I laughed.

Blaine leaned over the sleeping Mathieu and kissed me. "Always the smart one."

"Ewwww!" Mathieu shrieked, waking up and rubbing his eyes. Even at five he was already starting to get his daddy's accent and I loved hearing it come out of my other blond haired little boy.

"What? I can't be kissing your mama?" Blaine asked, tickling Mathieu, who curled up into a ball.

"Nooooo! That's my mama! Her kisses are only for me, Carter, and baby Grace," Mathieu said in his cute little accent.

"Well then, I might just have to tickle fight you to get my chance with her," Blaine said before digging into Mathieu, who squirmed and laughed.

"I'll defend your honor, brother!" Carter yelled and jumped on Blaine's back.

I moved out of the bed quickly, so I wasn't in the middle of another Crabtree boy wrestling match. They may have been rough, but I couldn't help but smile watching my little family. Though, it would be nice to have a girl.

"All right, boys, that's enough. We have to get ready and get to the shop."

"Are Grandma and Grandpa still coming?" Carter asked, hopping off the bed with his alligator footy pajamas hitting the hard wooden floor.

I nodded. "Yep. Maybe they brought you guys something from Chicago."

"Yes!" Carter pumped his fist in the air.

Blaine put his arm around me. "You know, I wouldn't be surprised if that boy ended up a Yankee and marrying some hoity Chicago girl."

I raised an eyebrow. "And would that be such a bad thing?"

Blaine laughed and kissed my forehead. "Nope. That just means he'll turn out like his daddy."

"Ew! I said no kissing you two!" Mathieu yelled.

Blaine laughed and put his hands up. "Okay, we'll stop kissing if you go in and brush your teeth and get dressed. Mama laid your clothes out for today."

"Aw, do I have to get all fancied up?" Mathieu moaned.

"Yes. If I have to, then you have to," Blaine said, pointing at the door.

Mathieu pouted, but left the room, followed closely by Carter.

"You ready for today?" Blaine asked, wrapping his arms around my waist.

"Ready as I think I'll ever be." I let out a deep breath of air.

He put his hand on my chin. "Hey. You know you've got this. It's just a formality for her to sign the shop over. You and Dina have been basically running this through two pregnancies, you finishing your bachelors, and me going to school and working. You're superwoman."

"I don't know about that." I smiled.

"How about a little fireball? Maybe a thunderstorm?" he asked.

I put my arms around his neck and leaned in, placing a small kiss on his lips. "Hmmm, I think I like you using weather analogies. What do I call you? My big hurricane?"

He smiled, pulling me closer. "If you're going to start talking like that, I may have to lock the door so the boys can't interrupt."

I kissed him again and again. "I doubt they would be gone long enough."

He slowly stepped back and locked the door. "I guess we can find out."

Blaine

I THOUGHT I WOULD HATE having a minivan. That it would take away some of my manliness. But with two kids in baseball, me coaching, and a third baby on the way, it was actually really reliable.

"And here he comes in his shagging wagon!" Jackson hollered as soon as we pulled up to the back of the shop.

I shook my head as I helped Carter out of his car seat. The kid was going to be a beast. I wouldn't be surprised if he was asking to wrestle and play football by the time kindergarten rolled around.

"You won't be saying that once your little girl is born and you're looking for a bigger vehicle," I yelled.

"Yeah, yeah!" He waved his hand off.

Libby took my hand with her free one and Mathieu held onto the other one. We walked together into the shop where Dee had a few papers set out and someone had made a cake. It was just the signing over of the shop, but really it was more than that.

It was the start of the official joining of Jackson's family and mine in a business venture. The start of Dee taking her time off that she so desperately needed.

"Hey, boys!" Libby's cousin Britt yelled and the boys let go of our hands, sprinting toward her.

"I thought you had practice?" Libby asked.

Britt fiddled with the hem of her dress black dress. The girl was definitely better suited out on the field, where she was now playing catcher for LSU with a full ride. "Yeah, but I couldn't miss the big day. It's great for you and Grandma."

"You know this means you're not getting out of coming home and working this summer when the season is over," Libby said.

Britt rolled her eyes. "Yeah, yeah!"

"Grandma! Grandpa!" Carter yelled, running through the store and into the arms of Libby's mom.

"Oh my goodness, you've gotten so big!" she carried him over to us as he nestled against her chest.

Libby's dad leaned in and kissed both boys, then hugged Libby before he shook my hand. "How's school going?"

"Almost done, sir. Just on my last few weeks of student teaching at Dupont."

"Does this mean we should start calling you Coach?" He raised his eyebrows.

I laughed, shaking my head. "Not yet."

Libby elbowed my side. "Oh yeah we can. Coach all but said he was retiring next year after you finish your first year as shop teacher at Elsbury."

"Is that true?" Jack asked.

I nodded and rubbed the back of my neck. "Yeah, sir. I guess it is."

He smiled for what seemed like the first time in his life. "We're proud of you, Blaine. You and Libby have really done some wonderful things."

"Thank you sir, I really appreciate it." And I meant it.

I looked over at Libby, who was talking to a very pregnant Dina.

It was as if she knew I was looking in her direction because immediately she turned toward me and grinned. The grin that could light up the whole room. The one that had since the moment I saw her.

I thought that by getting married, the paper walls surrounding me were going to close in and suffocate me. But really, those walls were just the beginning to putting up doors, windows, and new walls.

I may not have been able to go out with my friends on the weekends or taken a job in New Orleans, but those things weren't important anymore. Finding someone who took my paper heart that I thought was torn to shreds and made me whole again. Who made me fly, well, that was worth more than anything in the world.

"You ready to sign this paper and start the rest of our lives, Blaine?" Libby asked.

I smiled. "Of course."

If you enjoyed this book, please leave a review on GoodReads or whatever online retailer you picked up this book from.
It keeps the author happy and you get your own chance to be a writer :)

About the Author

Magan Vernon has been living off of reader tears since she wrote her first short story in 2004. She now spends her time killing off fictional characters, pretending to plot while she really just watches Netflix, and she tries to do this all while her two young children run amuck around her Texas ranch.

Sign up for her newsletter[1]

Or follow her Social Media

Facebook[2]

Reader Group[3]

Twitter[4]

GoodReads[5]

Pinterest[6]

Blog[7]

---

1. http://eepurl.com/qIJA5

2. http://www.facebook.com/pages/Author-Magan-Vernon/215620155165079

3. https://www.facebook.com/groups/VernonsVerses/

4. https://twitter.com/MaganVernon

5. http://www.goodreads.com/author/show/5237606.Magan_Vernon

6. http://pinterest.com/authormagan/

7. http://www.thepunchingbagfightsback.blogspot.com/

Acknowledgements

You would think, with this many books in, I'd have my acknowledgements down, but I always feel like I miss someone

A big shot out goes to my alpha Kelly Viel. Thank you for helping me to make this book one of the best of the series.

My PA, Alissa Glenn, what can I say? You're the best.

My husband, Timothy Ray, thanks for being the southern gentleman that inspired my Blaine.

Brandon Lane, thank you for being the perfect cover model. I didn't know there was a real Blaine out there until I saw you. You've been so helpful with everything!

Michael Meadows, you're my favorite. Don't tell my husband. You found me my Blaine. You found a place that looked like a bayou in Arizona! You're amazing!

Donna Dull, my cover designer. Thanks for putting up with my crazy demands!

Kellie Montgomery, I don't know how many aints there were, but I'm glad you don't hate me for them.

There are so many people that have helped this serious come into fruition and I feel like I'm forgetting so many, but know that I paper heart every single one of you!

Don't miss out!

Visit the website below and you can sign up to receive emails whenever Magan Vernon publishes a new book. There's no charge and no obligation.

https://books2read.com/r/B-A-ENHB-XPYG

BOOKS2READ

Connecting independent readers to independent writers.